About the author

Andrew Matthews bega⬚⬚⬚⬚⬚⬚⬚⬚⬚⬚⬚⬚⬚⬚⬚⬚⬚⬚ when he was
seven and had so much ⬚⬚⬚⬚⬚⬚⬚⬚⬚⬚⬚⬚ get to stop. He
has written over fifty books, many of which have been
translated into foreign languages.

Andrew's interests include reading, listening to music,
history and photography. He lives in Reading with his
wife and their two cats. The cats assist his writing by
lying over his notebooks and hiding pens under the
sofa in the lounge.

For Emily Lamb, to prove I keep promises

ORCHARD BOOKS

96 Leonard Street, London EC2A 4XD

Orchard Books Australia

32/45-51 Huntley Street, Alexandria, NSW 2015

ISBN 1 84362 077 4

First published in Great Britain in 2002

A paperback original

Text © Andrew Matthews 2002

The right of Andrew Matthews to be identified as the author of this work
has been asserted by him in accordance with
the Copyright, Designs and Patents Act, 1988.

A CIP catalogue record for this book is available from the British Library.

1 3 5 7 9 10 8 6 4 2

Printed in Great Britain

shadow
of the
wolf

ANDREW MATTHEWS

ORCHARD BOOKS

1

I was certain that I was over it; my tears had dried up, things were going OK with Nick, and I sometimes went as long as two hours without thinking about Simon. But two days before the end of summer term, Rose and I were on prefect-duty outside the Science Block at lunch-time, and suddenly there was Simon, coming towards me. Same tousled hair, soft brown eyes, mouth like a kiss it would be nice to be on the other side of – and I knew because I'd been there.

I had a mad flash: Simon had finally realised that I was the love of his life and he was going to beg me to take him back. Then I saw the bulging bag in his hand and sussed that he'd come to return his textbooks now that the GCSE exams were over. I went from deliriously happy to miserable in a nanosecond; so much for being over it!

Simon said, 'Hey, Danni! How you doing?'

'So-so,' I said. 'How did the exams go?'

'They went. I'm not going to think about them again until the day the results come out.'

This wasn't just talk. Simon had an amazing ability to shut out things, which had been a big part of our problem. I'd had ten incredible weeks with him just after I started Year Ten and he started Year Eleven, then he'd begun mumbling about exam pressure, revision and not seeing each other so often. It wasn't long before Simon gave me the let's-stay-friends speech and we weren't seeing each other at all. I was like – yeah, fine, cool – but how can you be friends with someone who makes you ache every time you meet?

'I'm off to the States tomorrow,' said Simon. 'Three weeks' travelling around. Can't wait!'

'Have a good time,' I said.

'I will. You too. See you.'

'See you,' I said, knowing that I wouldn't.

Simon went into the Science Block. Rose left a tactful gap before she said, 'You OK?'

'Sure! Why wouldn't I be?'

'Because you're still crazy about him.'

I almost denied it, but there wouldn't have been any

point. I could hide things from myself, but not from Rose.

'I can't help it,' I said. 'My head keeps telling me to let it go, but my heart won't listen.'

'And Nick?'

That was the million-pound question.

'Nick's all right,' I said.

Which was true, Nick *was* all right – sensitive, considerate, trustworthy – but there was no excitement, no carnival-ride feeling. I was in full control of the relationship, but it wasn't control that I needed. Nick was just there until someone more interesting came along.

'You're not being fair on Nick,' Rose said. 'You're using him as a substitute and he's going to wind up hurt. He really cares about you, you know?'

'That's not my fault. I didn't ask him to.'

'You didn't ask him not to either. Is this how it's going to be, Danni? Are you going to break hearts because Simon broke yours?'

'Of course not!'

'Then you'd better come clean to Nick before he gets in any deeper.'

I gave Rose a look.

'Know why you're my best mate?' I said.

'Why?'

'Because I can't afford to have you as an enemy. You know too much about my love life.'

Rose laughed her sunshine laugh.

'That's because I don't have a love life of my own,' she said.

That was something I'd never been able to figure. Rose was pretty, had personality plus, but couldn't get past the second date and had never been an item with anyone.

Rose needs a guy like Nick, I thought, and then the thought became an inspiration. Maybe there was a way of dumping Nick while simultaneously getting him together with Rose.

Nick appeared just before the end of lunch-break and brought me a bag of crisps and a can of Zing.

'Thought you could use these,' he said.

This was a typically thoughtful thing for Nick to do, but I turned up my nose.

'I'm off crisps,' I said. 'They give you zits. And I never drink Zing. Can't stand that chemically taste.'

Nick's shoulders sagged.

'Sorry,' he said.

'No need. You weren't to know.'

Nick cleared his throat nervously.

'Someone told me Simon was in school today,' he said.

'Yeah, I saw him a little while ago. He's going to the States tomorrow.'

'Lucky him!' said Nick, and he wasn't just talking about Simon's trip.

The bell went.

'Catch you later!' Nick said, and hurried off.

'How could you do that?' growled Rose.

'Do what?'

'Treat Nick like dirt when he was being so sweet. And what was all that guff about crisps? You pigged two bags yesterday.'

'Oh, I read this article about skincare in a mag last night,' I said, improvising.

'You could have taken them to be polite.'

'I don't do polite with Nick.'

'So I gathered. You don't know when you're well off, Danni.'

'I don't go for that romantic-gesture stuff. I'm not the chocolates-and-flowers type. I prefer a little danger.'

Rose blinked.

'You want a guy you can go mountain climbing with?' she said.

'I want a guy that matters so much it would hurt to lose him.'

Rose sighed and shook her head.

'Once wasn't enough for you, was it?' she said.

And I hated to admit it, but she was right.

When school finished I walked part of the way home with Rose. It was a hot, sticky afternoon, and there didn't seem to be any oxygen in the air.

'This weather sucks!' I grumbled.

'It'll soon change,' said Rose. 'As soon as the holiday starts, it'll pour with rain.'

'Remember when five weeks was a long time – like the summer holidays went on for ever?'

'And they were *proper* summers!' Rose said in her old-lady voice. 'Not like the summers you get nowadays.'

'What am I going to do about Nick, Rose?'

'You're going tell him, thanks, it's been fun but it isn't going anywhere. He hasn't done anything wrong, it's you. You're not ready for a steady relationship right now. You're not the special someone he's been looking for. That's what boys usually tell me anyway.'

I imagined telling Nick what Rose had said – the pain in his eyes, his mouth turning down at the edges. It would be like scolding a puppy.

'On the other hand I could ring him, say it's over and hang up,' I said.

'Don't you dare! The least he deserves is to be let down easy in person.'

'I guess.'

'You know what your problem is, Danni? You've been so busy comparing Nick to Simon that you forgot to find out who Nick is. You haven't given the poor guy a proper chance.'

'Keep it up, Rose!' I said. 'You're doing my self-esteem a power of good. According to you I'm a mean, selfish man-eater who enjoys leading boys on.'

'You left out the part about taking them for granted,' said Rose.

'Am I really that bad?'

'You will be if you don't snap out of it.'

Rose and I parted on the corner of Mayfield Avenue, and I carried on alone, full of depressing thoughts about myself. I decided to make Nick and Rose my pet project for the summer. Playing Cupid would prove there was some good in me. If I could talk Rose into providing Nick with a shoulder to cry on, I was halfway there.

I turned left into Hatford Crescent, which was slowly baking in the sunshine. It was completely deserted and still – even the leaves on the trees were too hot to move. All I wanted was to get home, change into shorts and a T-shirt and curl up inside the fridge until Mum came home from work.

As I stepped off the kerb to cross the road, I heard a weird noise, a buzzing, clicking sound, like a battery-operated toy. The noise stopped when I looked around. I expected to see a kid playing with a remote-controlled car, but there was nobody, just parked vehicles and houses rippling in the heat.

'Hearing things, Danni,' I murmured. 'Talking to yourself too. You must be cracking up.'

I thought I was in a bad way; I had no idea that things were about to get a lot worse.

2

That summer I had my first job, working weekday mornings at the local supermarket. It wasn't exactly demanding – I only had to stack shelves and be a gofer – but it was the only job I could get and I was grateful to have it. I figured it was going to be boring, but I'd be bored if I was stuck at home, and at least the supermarket was paying me for my boredom.

On my first day I made a lot of cups of coffee for various supervisors, loaded a batch of warm baguettes on to their rack in the baking department, and got to know more about washing powder and cat food than I knew there was to know. I also found out that supermarket work is murder on the feet. Then, as I was pushing a trolley filled with empty cat-food boxes to the waste disposal area, I clocked one of my fellow employees filling a chest freezer with bags of frozen vegetables.

He was my age or a bit older, gangly, with longish black hair and green eyes. His spectacles were a little nerdy and he was wearing the overalls we all had to wear – in an unfetching shade of brown that was never going to be the new black – but there was something about him. I had him down as one of those shy, bookish types who have no idea that they're attractive.

He sensed that someone was watching him, looked up and our eyes met.

I gave him a smile and said, 'Hi.'

He said, 'Hi,' blushed and went back to filling the freezer.

I put a tick in the 'shy' box and congratulated myself on being a shrewd judge of character.

I didn't see the boy again until later. I knocked-off work at half twelve, feeling that the rest of the day was mine and I'd earned it. The weather was hot and sunny, and I was planning an afternoon's tanning. I walked beside the low wall around the supermarket car park, passed a guy who had his face buried in a book, then did a double-take, because it was the frozen vegetable boy.

Tick in the 'bookish' box and another slap on the back.

'Hello,' I said. 'You finished for the day?'

The boy squinted at me.

'No,' he said. 'This is my lunch-break. I'm on again at half one.'

'I'm Danni. I work part time. Started this morning.'

'David,' said the boy. 'I've been here three weeks.'

I did the sums. He'd been working at the supermarket while I was still at school, so his term must have ended before mine.

'Are you a university student?' I said.

'No. I've just finished my GCSEs.'

'Which school d'you go to?'

'St Joseph's College.'

I'd heard of it. St Joseph's regularly thrashed Temple Street Comp at sports meets.

'I thought it was a boarding school,' I said.

'They take day pupils as well, and before you ask, no, my parents aren't rich or posh. I won a scholarship.'

I guessed the other pupils at St Joseph's gave him stick for this, which accounted for his slightly aggressive tone.

'I take my GCSEs next summer,' I said. 'Any tips?'

'Yeah, don't leave your revision to the last minute.'

I stuck out my bottom lip, blew air up over my face and sat on the wall, next to David.

'It's hot, isn't it?' I said.

'Summers are famous for it.'

That stymied me on a conversation about the weather, so I said, 'What are you reading?'

'A book,' said David.

'Well, duh! I can see that. What's it about?'

David turned the book round to show me the title on the cover: *Advanced Darkroom Techniques.*

'You into photography?' I said.

'No, I just enjoy reading about it.'

'But your real hobby is being sarcastic, right?'

David's cheeks reddened.

'I didn't mean—' he said.

I stood up.

'It's OK,' I said. 'I can tell when I'm not welcome.'

I walked ten paces before David came running up behind me.

'Look, I'm sorry,' he said. 'I'm not normally so touchy. I've got a lot on my mind at the moment and I shouldn't have taken it out on you.'

I could tell what he had on his mind. There was a

look in his eyes that said 'girl trouble'.

'I'll survive,' I said.

David put out his right hand.

'Friends?' he said.

I took his hand, shook it and said, 'Not yet, but maybe.'

David smiled. It was a nice smile, but there was a fence of caution around it.

'Buy you a drink as a peace offering?' he said.

I hesitated. If I accepted it would mean more talk, getting to know each other better and a whole bunch of stuff I might not want to get into.

'I promise not to bite,' David said.

The way he said it made me laugh, and I thought, ah, why not?

We went to the café in the precinct, directly opposite the supermarket. There were tables and chairs set outside, which made it feel continental until you sat down and realised you only had the precinct to look at.

David was tense, embarrassed that we'd got off to such a bad start.

To try and relax him, I said, 'So what's the deal with photography? You just point the camera and shoot, don't you?'

'That's what most people do, and then they moan about the results.'

'Tell me about it!' I said. 'I hate having my picture taken. I never look like me in photos.'

'You have to know somebody to take a good picture of them,' said David. 'People are constantly changing their expression. You have to wait until they're wearing the right face. Plus, you're used to the way you look in a mirror. Mirrors reverse left and right. In a photograph, you're the right way around.'

'And it makes a difference?'

'Sure. Nobody's face is perfect. Look at mine – the left side is a fraction higher than the right.'

I looked, and it was true.

'Actually, I'm more interested in developing photographs than taking them,' David went on. 'You drop a blank sheet of paper into a tray of chemicals, sloosh it around and an image condenses. It's like magic.'

He told me a lot more that went right over my head, but his enthusiasm was magnetic, and all of a sudden we'd been talking for twenty minutes and David's lunch-break was almost over.

'You ought to bring some of your pictures into work

to show me,' I said.

'I wouldn't want to bore you.'

'I won't be bored.'

'I'm not that good yet.'

'Oh, I get it!' I said. 'You wind me up about photography and then leave me flat. That's no way to treat an impressionable young girl.'

David frowned.

'Are you trying to lay a guilt-trip on me?' he said.

'Uh-huh.'

'If I don't bring any photographs to show you, you're going to nag me till I do, aren't you?'

'Certainly am. You might as well give in. It'll save you an ear bashing.'

'Do you always get your own way?'

'No,' I said, 'but I keep trying.'

Walking home, I had that buzz you get from meeting someone new and feeling a current of mutual liking flow between you. I wasn't scheming how I could get my mucky paws on David or anything, it was just nice to know that there was someone on the staff of the supermarket that I could talk to. If he turned out to be a camera anorak, it would be easy to ditch him – or so I thought.

When I got in, I stood in the hall for a moment, enjoying the cool gloom, then I spotted the blinking light on the answer-phone. I pressed *PLAY* and the display told me there were two messages.

The first was from Nick.

'Hi, Danni. I was hoping we could get together tonight. I'll call you later.'

The second message was puzzling: thirty seconds of silence followed by the clatter of a receiver being replaced.

'Wrong number,' I thought, but thirty seconds was a long time to wait before hanging up. The person who'd called must have known that they'd made a mistake as soon as they heard the voice on the answering-machine. Why hadn't they put the phone down straight away?

The question bothered me for a minute or two, but I quickly forgot about it because I had far more important things on my mind.

Like Nick, for instance.

3

I tried to sunbathe on the back lawn, but I couldn't settle. I kept thinking about Nick, and my thoughts didn't make me feel particularly good about myself. Rose had been right, I'd used Nick to get over Simon. Nick had been my ego-boost, because no matter how badly I treated him he always bounced back for more – Nick, the human rubber ball. I wasn't being fair to him, and it was gradually turning me into the sort of person that I couldn't stand. The best thing to do was to make a clean break, only I knew that the kind of break I had to make wouldn't be clean; there would be ragged edges, like there always are when you finish with someone.

I went into the house, rang Nick's number and lucked in – he picked up straight away, but didn't sound as happy to hear from me as he usually did.

'You OK?' I asked.

'Yeah,' said Nick. 'Can we meet somewhere? There's something I have to tell you.'

'Memorial Park, three o' clock?'

'I'll be there.'

It was only after I'd hung up that I remembered the significance of Memorial Park. It was where Nick had first asked me out, where we'd first kissed, now it was going to be the place where I dumped him. My chances of winning the Miss Tactful award took a steep dive.

I dressed down, in baggy shorts, flip-flops and my oldest T-shirt, and tied back my hair in the way I knew didn't suit my face, hoping that Nick would register what a mess I was and be glad to get shot of me. The heat helped; by the time I reached the park I was dripping with sweat and there were wet blotches on my top.

Nick was waiting at the park gates, looking ridiculously cool in a tennis shirt and shorts.

'What is it with you?' I asked resentfully. 'How come you're immaculate and I'm melting?'

'The heat doesn't bother me,' Nick said with a shrug.

It wasn't the kind of reply I was used to from Nick –

in fact I couldn't remember the last thing he'd said to me that hadn't been an apology.

We walked slowly through the park, past beds of wilting flowers. Nick was quiet and didn't look at me.

'So what did you drag me all the way out here to tell me?' I said.

'It's over, isn't it?' said Nick. 'I don't make you happy any more.'

He took me by surprise, and I scrambled to regain my balance so that I could stay in control.

'It's not you, Nick, it's us,' I said. 'We don't make each other happy.'

'We might have if you'd given us a chance.'

This was true enough to make me wince.

'Maybe,' I said.

'I can't be Simon. I gave it my best shot, but I can only be me.'

'What does Simon have to do with it?'

'Everything. You still care about him more than you care about me. I don't want to settle for second best, and nor should you.'

I was starting to feel uncomfortable; Nick obviously understood me a lot better than I'd thought.

'Don't bring Simon into this,' I said. 'It's a you-and-me thing. You're a great guy, Nick, and some day you'll meet someone and have something really special, but not with me. I'm not ready for a long-term relationship, and I was a bitch to let you think I was. The last thing I wanted was to hurt your feelings, but—'

Nick laughed.

'Oh, please, let's be honest shall we, Danni?' he said. 'I got you on the rebound and I thought that if I hung on in there for long enough, you'd let Simon go. My mistake. Now it's time we moved on.'

Nick had turned things inside-out. I'd come to Memorial Park with a bunch of carefully-selected clichés that were meant to let him down easy, and he'd beaten me to it. Nick was more perceptive than I'd given him credit for, and it struck me that if he'd spoken his mind at the start, we wouldn't be in this situation.

'I'm sorry it has to end like this,' I said.

'No you're not, Danni. You're relieved because I've let you off the hook. You've been wondering how to dump me for weeks.'

'Can we stay friends?'

I couldn't have said anything more lame, and Nick

gave me the scornful snort I deserved.

'We've never been friends, Danni,' he said. 'Friends open up and tell each other stuff. I wasn't important enough to you for you to trust me.'

'Can we try and make friends?'

'Not while I've got hurting to do.'

'You must hate me,' I said.

'It's not that simple. I'm disappointed, and sad, and angry with myself for acting like a jerk, but I don't hate you. I'm not the hating kind.'

I tried to salvage some self-respect.

'You know, it's funny,' I said. 'I was thinking the other day – you're a nice guy, Rose is a nice girl, wouldn't it be terrific if—?'

'Don't patronise me!' Nick snapped.

'What?'

'Did you figure you could pass me on to Rose, like a toy you don't want to play with any more? No thanks, Danni! I'll make my own decisions about who I get involved with, if it's all the same to you.'

'I'm sorry, Nick,' I said; it was all that I had left to say.

'Me too,' said Nick. 'It's partly my fault. I wanted you to be my ideal girl so much that I forgot people are real. I won't do that again in a hurry.'

'I know I have no right to ask you, but will you do me a favour, Nick?'

'It depends.'

'Will you go on telling me the truth, especially when I'm being up myself?'

Nick smiled, like friendship might just be possible.

'You've got it,' he said; then he stiffened and his face changed.

I said, 'Nick?'

Nick's voice dropped to a whisper.

'Someone's watching us,' he said. 'Can you feel it?'

I couldn't feel anything.

'They're in those bushes behind you,' said Nick. 'Turn around slowly and take a look.'

I turned and as I did, I thought I heard a faint scuffle and the snap of a dry twig.

'They've gone,' Nick said.

'Who was it?'

'Don't know. Probably kids.'

I had a flash of déja vu, like the echo of a memory or a dream, but when I tried to pin it down, it slipped away.

I shuddered.

'Are you cold?' said Nick.

'Spooked. Who'd want to spy on us?'

'Maybe they were admiring what a lovely couple we make,' said Nick.

The fact that he could be ironic about it meant that he was already on the mend.

I was home by five. I flopped in the lounge, turned on the TV and channel-hopped, searching for something mindless because thinking didn't seem like a good idea. Nick had made me take a hard look at myself, and I hadn't liked what I'd seen. The idea that I might have deliberately set Nick up to hurt him the way that Simon had hurt me wasn't pleasant, and I shied away from it like a horse refusing a jump.

I'd just got into some sword-and-sorcery saga, when the phone rang. I groaned at the interruption and went into the hall to answer.

'Hello?' I said.

No reply.

'Hello? Who's calling please?'

I could hear breathing, the sound of passing traffic.

'Which number were you trying to call?' I said.

The person on the other end of the line hung up.

Just for a second I had the crazy idea that the phone call was connected with what had happened in

Memorial Park, that whoever had been watching me and Nick had rung me.

Then I thought, get real, Danni! Who'd go to that kind of bother, and what for?

I returned to the lounge and the junky TV programme.

4

Next morning I really got on top of the supermarket job, making sure that my shelves were stacked neatly and that all the labels on the tins and packets were facing the same way. Sounds saddo, I know, but it was my way of making a boring chore meaningful.

I ran into David mid-morning, at the end of the pet food aisle. He grinned and said, 'Well, you talked me into it. I brought in some pictures to show you. I thought we could go back to that café in my lunch-break.' His face worked shiftily. 'And I wondered if you'd mind—'

That's when Mary pounced. Mary was one of the supervisors, and she took her supervision seriously. She peered down her nose at David and said, 'Shouldn't you be in the stockroom?'

'I'm on my way,' said David. 'I was just having a

quick word with Danni.'

'And it couldn't wait till your break? You're not being paid to chat, you know.'

David slunk off, and it was my turn.

'As for you, Danni,' Mary said, 'I suggest that you restrict your flirting to your own time, is that clear?'

I was about to protest that I hadn't been flirting, but Mary's expression told me that I'd better not.

It made me think though. As far as I was concerned, I was being friendly to David because he was the only interesting person on the staff, but how did he see it: as a come on? I'd have to be more careful about what kind of messages I gave out.

At lunch-time, David and I sat outside the café and he gave me a photo album to look at. Some of the pics were corny – sunsets and cats; some were self-consciously arty – smeary reflections on a wet pavement, the arm of a shop-dummy poking out of a dustbin. The best were the ones of people, particularly a head-and-shoulders portrait of a girl gazing straight into the camera. She was smiling, but there was an uncertainty in her eyes that made her seem vulnerable.

'This is terrific,' I said. 'Who's the model?'

David wriggled.

'That's Kate,' he said. 'We were an item for a while.'

'How long a while?'

'A year.'

David said it so casually that I sussed he'd given it a lot of practice.

'Still hurting?' I said.

'Only when I think about her, which is most of the time.'

'Been out with anyone else since?'

'Once or twice. It didn't work out.'

'I know what you mean,' I said. 'The Kate in my life is called Simon.'

We swapped tales of true-life heartache. I kept mine low-key, but when David told his story, a note of bitterness crept into his voice.

'I totally trusted her,' he said. 'I told her things about myself that I'd never told anybody, and she betrayed me. I'm not going to be caught like that again. I'm going to make sure that I'm the one who calls the shots.'

I had a severe attack of déja vu. Listening to David was like listening to me talk about my relationship with Nick. A wave of shame went over me and I blushed.

'Being in control isn't the answer,' I said. 'You can

hurt someone without meaning to.'

'Yeah? In my book, hurting beats being hurt.'

'I used to think that way. I don't any more. Hurting people doesn't make you feel good about yourself.'

David shrugged.

'Enough about exes already,' he said. 'I've got a proposition for you.'

'Oh?'

I tensed because I was afraid that he was about to ask me for a date.

'How about I take the best photograph of you that's ever been taken?'

I laughed in relief. 'So, you're a guy who likes challenges?'

'I like your face. It's intriguing.'

It struck me as a strange word to choose to describe a face, especially mine.

'I've been trying for pretty, or gorgeous,' I said. 'But I guess that intriguing will have to do.'

David reached into the pocket of his jeans and took out a camera the size of a cigarette pack.

'This is my new toy,' he said. 'It's digital. The quality's not quite as good as film, but it's close.'

I didn't have a clue what he was talking about.

David raised the camera to his face, and I got twitchy. The blank eye of the lens made me feel clumsy and self-conscious.

'What should I do?' I asked.

'Relax, for a start. You're tense.'

'What else would I be with that thing pointing at me?'

'Don't worry, it's not going to steal your soul. Turn your head sideways and forget that I'm here.'

I did as he asked.

The camera went *whirr-click, whirr-click*.

I recognised the sound immediately. I'd heard it before, in Hatford Crescent on the last day of term. It hadn't been a kid playing with a battery-operated toy; someone had taken pictures of me.

My imagination went into overdrive, turning illogical ideas into a half-baked conspiracy theory. Had it been David in Hatford Crescent, photographing me? Had he made the phone call? Was this some kind of twisted revenge on all girls in general, for being dumped by Kate?

I was thinking irrationally, sliding into paranoia, but I couldn't stop myself. I couldn't let this go without being absolutely certain.

David said, 'What's the matter? You've gone stiff.'

'Ever taken pictures of a girl walking home from school?'

The hardness in my voice made David frown.

'What?' he said.

'Ever hidden in a street you know she'll walk down, so you can snap her on the sly?'

'What are you talking about, Danni?'

'I don't enjoy having my privacy invaded.'

David's frown deepened.

'I'm not invading your privacy,' he said, 'just taking a couple of shots of you, that's all. No big deal. If you have some kind of a problem with it, forget it. I didn't mean to hassle you.'

I knew I was in danger of making a fool of myself, but I was too wound up to care. I got to my feet and said, 'This was a bad idea. I'm sorry. I have to go now.'

I walked away.

David called out, 'Danni?'

I ignored him.

All the way home I was convinced that someone was tailing me, but I wouldn't look over my shoulder to check, because it would have been giving in to my attack of the jitters. I was probably wrong about

David, but if he hadn't taken my picture in Hatford Crescent, who had?

I needed a reality check, so as soon as I got in I rang Rose. We talked about nothing much, then I said, 'Rose, has anybody said anything to you about me?'

'What kind of thing?'

'Nasty stuff.'

'Why would they?'

'Oh, I don't know. Maybe because Nick and I split up.'

'When was this?'

'Yesterday. I've had some weird phone calls. D'you know someone who has it in for me?'

'You're not Michaela Robson's favourite person.'

That was putting it mildly. Michaela was Nick's old girlfriend, and even though it was over between them ages before he got together with me, Michaela had made a point of spreading goss about how mean I was to him.

'Would Michaela try to freak me out?' I said.

'Only in front of a large audience,' said Rose. 'You know what a drama queen she is.'

Rose had a point.

Later on, I told my parents about the calls. Mum

was concerned; Dad reacted with his usual logical calm.

'And the caller didn't say anything?' he said. 'No threats or obscenities?'

'No, but I could feel that someone was there. It was creepy.'

'It's probably kids mucking about. If it happens again, we'll get the phone company to monitor our number. It's important for you not to react. Nuisance callers get their kicks from upsetting their victims.'

'If I find out who it is, they'll get kicks all right,' I said. 'Right in the butt.'

'Should we contact the police?' asked Mum.

Dad shook his head.

'There's no point at this stage,' he said. 'The police couldn't do any more than we can do ourselves. Don't pick up the phone when you're on your own, Danielle. Let the answering-machine deal with it.'

But as I was to discover, leaving a ringing phone unanswered was easier said than done.

5

For the next few days everything quietened down –
apart from me, that is. There were no more weird
phone calls, but whenever I was alone in the house,
I kept expecting the phone to ring, and it kept me
on edge. David steered well clear of me at work,
which suited me fine, because I didn't know how to
go about apologising to him, and I also didn't know
if he deserved an apology. I caught him gazing at me
across the supermarket once or twice, and I couldn't
figure out what the expression in his eyes meant.
Was he reproaching me because I'd hurt his feelings,
or was it the glassy stare of someone with an
unhealthy obsession?

Then, on Friday, the world unravelled.

I took my break at eleven o' clock and went to the
staff room to make myself a cup of coffee. There was

no one else around when I got there, but as I was filling my mug with hot water from the electric kettle, I heard the door go. I turned and saw David. He held out an envelope and mumbled, 'Peace offering.'

Cautiously, I took the envelope. It felt like there was a greetings card inside, but when I opened it I found two photographs of me sitting outside the café in the precinct. The first was a profile shot, the second was full-face. David must have taken it just after I registered the sound his camera made. I looked shocked and terrified, like a nocturnal animal trapped in the headlights of a car, uncertain whether to stay put or bolt.

'Why have you given me these?' I said.

David blushed.

'To show that I don't think your face belongs to me,' he said. 'I deleted the pictures from my computer. Those are the only copies.'

He'd told me that the camera wouldn't steal my soul, but it had. My fear had been captured and turned into an image.

My skin crawled.

'Does taking pictures of people when they're scared get you off?' I said.

'No! I just thought—'

'Do me a favour, David,' I said. 'Back off, and in future, don't think about me at all, OK?'

I walked out on him before he could reply, shut myself in a cubicle in the loos and had a shivering fit that lasted for five minutes.

At knocking-off time I slipped away and ran smack into Situation Number Two, because Greg Hastings was waiting outside the staff entrance.

Greg was one of the guys who hung out with Nick at school. I knew that Greg had a thing for me, because he'd made jokes about it in a way that showed he meant it.

'Hi, Danni!' he said. 'How's the world of work?'

'Fine,' I said. 'Look, Greg, I'm in a bit of a—'

'I hear you and Nick split up. That right?'

I sighed. I obviously wasn't going to get rid of Greg in a hurry.

'Yes,' I said. 'News travels fast, doesn't it?'

'Did you split up with him, or did he split up with you?'

'It was mutual.'

'So...you're not going out with anyone at the moment? I've been meaning to give you a call during the week, but—'

I flipped.

'Did you ring me up the other day and then put down the phone without saying anything?' I said.

'Huh?'

'Have you been following me around with a camera?'

Greg shook his head.

'What are you on about?' he said.

'Greg, why don't you do us both a favour and leave me alone?'

I left him gawping, like a fish in the bottom of a boat.

On the way home I was scared and furious. When it comes to a choice between fight and flight, I'm a fighter, and right then I was all geared-up for fighting, but I didn't know my enemy was. That was why I'd given Greg a mauling. I had no reason to think that he was the person who'd been stalking me, but there was no reason to think he wasn't either, and I was in full guilty-until-proven-innocent mode. The worst part was that I was losing control of my life and myself. The stalker could yank my chain any time, and there was nothing I could do about it.

As I opened the front door, the phone rang, startling me. I let it ring, trying to resist answering, but I couldn't. If it was my mystery caller, they were going to get a right earful.

I picked up the phone and said, 'Hello?'

'Danni, it's David. What did I do wrong?'

'Nothing.'

'Are you sure? Like at the beginning of the week you were friendly and we got along well, and this morning you were—'

'There's some stuff I have to get sorted.'

'If I offended you, then—'

My brain was zapping all over the place.

'David,' I said, 'where did you get my number?'

'I sweet-talked a supervisor into letting me take a peek at your application form.'

My application form: name, date of birth, address, telephone number, contact numbers for my parents and doctor – how many other people had sweet-talked the supervisor? Information about me was everywhere – forms, computer files, school, medical and dental records. Finding things out wouldn't be difficult for someone who was determined enough. My entire life was public property, and I had nowhere to hide.

'You had no right to do that!' I said.

'I know, but I couldn't leave things as they were. You're a tough girl to figure. I, um, really like you, Danni.'

Admirers were crawling out of the woodwork wherever I looked. I ought to have felt flattered, but it was kind of eerie, like everyone was watching me.

'I don't need to hear this, David,' I said. 'Another time, another place, but not here and now, OK?'

Somehow I got rid of David before he got too sticky, and I went upstairs for a cold shower. I'd just about put on my shorts, when the doorbell rang. Afternoon callers are seldom good news, and I was grumbling under my breath as I opened the door.

A young woman was on the doorstep, dressed in smart designer clothes, must-have Ray-Bans pushed up into her sleek golden-brown hair. She had a funky feathered cut with short layers at the front that framed her face. Her skin was pale and smooth and her make-up was so classy that she didn't appear to be wearing any.

She gave me a blindingly white smile and said, 'Hello, Danni. It's been a long time, hasn't it?'

Her voice was confident, bright and upper class.

'I'm sorry,' I said. 'Do I know you?'

The smile widened.

'Oh, yes,' the young woman said. 'We used to know each other very well. We were close friends.'

The darkness in her eyes gave her away. Dreams and memories tumbled through my mind in an avalanche, and suddenly I was nine years old again, standing on Memorial Road.

'*Leah?*' I gasped.

6

I'd met Leah Warner on her first day at Temple Street Juniors. We couldn't help meeting. Miss Penhaligan made us sit together, and told me to look after Leah until she knew her way around.

I was wary because Leah was...well, different. She was a head taller than the other girls in the class, and sturdy with it – not fat, but large. She had curly brown hair and a long, boyish face. The most striking thing about her was her eyes. They were pale brown, almost yellow, and kept flicking from side to side, like the eyes of an antelope that knows a pride of lions is hidden in the long grass.

Her shy nervousness made me feel sorry for her and I decided to play mother hen, take her under my wing and impress her with what a cool and considerate person I was.

So, come morning break, I tagged along behind Leah and followed her outside. The weather was finer than it had been all summer. Dozens of kids surged across the playground, shouting and laughing.

Then – WHAM! – Leah wheeled around and snapped, 'What d'you want?'

Her eyes weren't anxious any more, they were wild and threatening. I noticed her fingers curl into fists.

'N-nothing!' I squeaked.

'Then why are you following me?'

'I'm not!' I said. 'I'm just walking in the same direction as you. What d'you think of Miss Penhaligan? She's nice, isn't she?'

Leah's fingers uncurled.

'I suppose,' she said.

'I was dead scared when I first came here,' I said. 'I had nightmares about big kids sticking my head down the loo and flushing it. But I reckon that's just a story people tell to wind you up. I mean, have you ever met anybody who's had their head stuck down a loo?'

'Yeah,' said Leah. 'You always like this?'

'Like what?'

'You always talk a lot?'

I blushed.

'Sorry,' I said.

'No need,' said Leah. 'I like it.'

'You're not from round here, are you?'

I didn't mean anything by the comment, I was only making conversation, but the darkness came back into Leah's eyes.

'What d'you mean?' she said. 'How did you know? Who told you?'

'No one. I can tell by your accent. You're from London, aren't you?'

I could see Leah weighing-up whether to answer or not.

'Right,' she said finally.

'What part of London?'

'I'm not an East Ender, if that's what you're thinking.'

'When did you move to Frinley?'

'In the summer. My dad's the manager of the Grey Horse Inn. D'you know it?'

'That's the pub in Walker Road, isn't it?' I said. 'I was born here. I mean, not at the school, in Frinley. It must seem quiet after London.'

'I like quiet places,' said Leah.

We didn't say a lot after that, but at the end of the day

I spotted Leah waiting at the school gate. Her head was down, like she didn't want to be noticed. I was going to walk over to her, but just then a black car with tinted windows pulled up beside the gate, and Leah got in.

It struck me as odd: I'd thought that only famous people drove cars with tinted windows, or people with something to hide.

Two days later, I had a reminder of what a nasty place Temple Street School could be. A Year Six girl, Becky Tillotson, took a dislike to me – I still don't know why – and picked on me at morning break. I was sitting on a bench, swigging OJ and minding my own business, and a voice said, 'What you doing, *kid*?'

I turned my head and saw Becky smirking down at me. Two other girls were with her and they were smirking too.

'I'm not doing anything,' I said.

'Oh yes you are!' said Becky. 'This is *our* bench, kid, so shift your butt.'

I stood up to go, but the three girls closed in on me and started pushing me this way and that.

'Look at her!' said Becky. 'Doesn't know whether she's coming or going, does she?'

Then a hand clamped down on Becky's shoulder and yanked her backwards. The other girls stepped aside and I saw Leah, standing so close to Becky that their noses almost touched.

'Leave her alone!' Leah said.

I'd never seen anybody look so furious, and I don't think that Becky had either. She registered how big Leah was – a good three centimetres taller than Becky – and lost her nerve.

'Come on,' she said to her friends. 'Let's go somewhere else. It smells here!'

The three girls turned their backs on us and slinked away.

'Thank you,' I said.

'I hate bullies!' said Leah, curling her top lip and showing her teeth. 'Are you OK?'

'Yes.'

'If they pick on you again just let me know,' said Leah.

And I realised that I'd made a friend.

7

I came out of the long memory-flash, blinking like a cartoon mole.

Leah laughed at my astonishment.

'I haven't changed that much, have I?' she said.

'You've changed completely. Your hair is—'

Leah shrugged.

'I had it straightened,' she said. 'Curly hair made me look far too young.'

'And what happened to your accent?'

'Boarding school. My parents move frequently, so it's less disruptive for my education. And state schools vary so much in quality, don't they?'

The shock of seeing Leah wore off enough for me to remember my manners.

'Come in,' I said.

'Are you sure it's convenient? If you're going

somewhere, I could call another time. I happened to be in the area and thought I might call in on the off chance that you still lived here.'

'I'm not going anywhere,' I said. 'To tell you the truth, I could use some company.'

We went into the lounge. Leah looked around, smiling.

'You've redecorated,' she said. 'The walls were green last time I saw them, weren't they?'

'That's right. Do sit down.'

Leah took the armchair near the front window, moving like a ballerina. I'd never seen anyone sit down so gracefully.

'I have such fond memories of this place,' Leah said. 'How are your parents?'

'Both well.'

'I'm glad to hear it. They were always so kind to me. Every time I visited you, I felt like one of the family.'

As far as I could recall, Leah had only visited the house once, and that had been when—

Leah's voice cut through the memory.

'I used to envy you, you know,' she said. 'This house had a welcoming atmosphere, like a real home.'

'How's your family?'

Leah rolled her eyes.

'As chaotic as ever. Sean's staying with friends in the south of France this summer – thank goodness!'

'You two don't get on, I gather.'

'We never did, did we? We don't see each other that often. If we did, I think I might have throttled my darling baby brother long ago.'

'And your mum and dad?'

'They're fine. They live in Spain. Dad owns a bar on the Costa del something-or-other.'

I couldn't get over how poised and elegant the new Leah was. There was no trace left of the galumphing schoolgirl I'd known, and her crystal-cut accent never slipped.

'Would you like a coffee or something?' I said.

'I wouldn't mind a cup of camomile tea, if you have any.'

'Sorry.'

'Or a glass of Icelandic water.'

'Icelandic water?' I said, thinking it was a joke.

'Iceland has the purest water in Europe,' Leah said solemnly. 'I'm on a health-kick at the moment. My beautician tells me that my skin is inclined to be oily, and I suffer from blocked pores if I'm not careful about what I eat and drink.'

I felt so thoroughly put in my place that I almost apologised for the quality of the refreshments on offer. I slouched on the sofa and noticed Leah's body language: knees together, hands crossed in her lap; perched on the edge of the chair as though she were about to leap up and lope off at any second.

'How come you left Frinley in such a hurry?' I said.

Leah pursed her lips.

'The brewery withdrew my father's contract,' she said. 'They gave us a month's notice.'

'You knew you had to leave and you didn't say anything?'

'Didn't I?' Leah said with a frown. 'I was probably in denial and couldn't face telling you. I've always hated saying goodbye, especially to close friends, and you and I were as close as sisters, weren't we? You were the last of my childhood. I never found another friend like you afterwards. Of course, I had a lot of unresolved emotional issues back then – anxiety and that kind of thing.'

I recognised therapy-speak when I heard it, and guessed that Leah had undergone a course of treatment.

'Anxiety about what?' I said.

'The situation I found myself in. The best way I can explain is to say that I found some of my parents' business associates rather intimidating. I probably got things completely out of proportion.' Leah waved her hand as though brushing a fly away. 'But I didn't come here to talk about myself. Do you still see any of our old crowd?'

This was pushing it, as we'd been a crowd of two.

'Just Rose,' I said.

There was no mistaking the flash of annoyance in Leah's eyes.

'Rose?' she said.

'Rose Palmer – the girl you threatened to beat up because she'd made friends with me?'

'I did? That doesn't sound like me.'

'You were like that then,' I said.

'What a horrible person I must have been.'

'Not horrible. Jealous, maybe.'

'And terribly lonely,' said Leah. 'That's why I was so grateful for your friendship.'

Leah was harping on about the friendship thing, and it didn't add up.

I said, 'Why didn't you stay in touch?'

'Oh, you know how it is when you move house and make a fresh start. I thought a complete break would be best, and I'm afraid I'm not a great one for writing letters.'

'Where are you living now?'

'With relatives. Not far away.'

'Boyfriends?' I said.

Good choice: Leah rattled on for ten minutes straight about Marty, a guy she'd met in a London club. He was an American university student, studying in Britain as part of an exchange scheme.

'We had six brilliant months together, then he had to go back to the States,' Leah concluded. 'How about your love life?'

'What love life?' I said. 'When it comes to boys, I'm a mess.'

'Really?' said Leah, sounding surprised. 'I find that hard to believe.'

To make it easier for her to believe, I treated her to the saga of Simon and Nick. She made been-there-done-that noises in the right places, and I was impressed with her listening skills; she seemed to be drinking in every detail.

'Poor Danni!' she said when I'd finished. 'Boys

always want too much, don't they?'

'Or not enough.'

Leah glanced at her watch and sighed.

'The time's gone so quickly,' she said. 'There's so much more I'd like to know, but if I don't leave soon I'll miss my train.'

She'd placed the ball so subtly in my court that I automatically said, 'How are you fixed for tomorrow? I could meet you in town and show you how much of it's still standing.'

Leah beamed. 'That would be terrific. Outside the station at half eleven? We could do lunch somewhere.'

'OK, but I can't guarantee any Icelandic water.'

I showed Leah out. Just before she turned to go, she said, 'It's been lovely to talk to you again.'

'Me too. Thanks for coming over.'

Leah leaned forward and kissed me on the cheek and I heard her sniff rapidly, like a dog taking a scent.

'You smell just the same as you used to,' she said. 'Take care, Danni.'

After Leah left, more memories came back. They were patchy and jumbled, and it was difficult to work out how many were real and how many I'd imagined. I'd buried Leah deep inside myself, and though a part of me said that she ought to stay buried, an even stronger part of me wanted to know why.

8

You don't worry about friends when you're a kid, do you? You take it for granted that people will get on with you. It's only later, when you hit your teens, that the doubts leak in. You think, *Why* do people like me? What's to like? Do I even like myself? But with Leah and me it was straightforward, or so I thought.

We got to know each other better, or rather Leah got to know me, because I was the one who did the talking. She told me hardly anything about herself, but I was too busy chuntering for it to really register.

I helped her in lessons. She always got there in the end, but I was quicker when it came to picking up on things. I wasn't quicker than her at games though: Leah could out-run, out-jump and out-swim every girl in the class, and most of the boys as well.

'D'you work out?' I asked her once.

'Mum and Dad train at a gym one night a week,' said Leah. 'They drop Sean and me at an activities club. We like to keep fit. You never know when it'll come in handy.'

'In handy for what?'

Leah clammed. It was her most irritating habit; she had a way of ignoring a question that left you wondering if you'd actually asked it.

Our contact was limited to school. I invited Leah over to my place a few times, but she always seemed to have something on with her family, and I gave up in the end. I didn't think there was anything weird about it, it was just how things were between us.

And then one morning in late November, Leah said, 'Mum and Dad want to meet you.'

'Sorry?' I said.

'Mum and Dad want to meet you. Can you come to tea some time this week?'

'Sure,' I said.

'Tomorrow?'

'I'll have to ask my parents.'

I was excited because meeting Leah's family would give me a chance to find out more about her and take our friendship up a level. I didn't notice until later that

Leah seemed less than enthusiastic.

My folks gave me the OK, so next day, after lessons finished, I joined Leah at the school gate. She was even more quiet than usual. I realise now that she was anxious and brooding, but at the time I thought she was being sulky, so I tried to lighten her mood.

'Funny, isn't it – going to a pub to have tea?' I said.

'Don't pay any attention to them,' said Leah.

'Who?'

'Mum and Dad are a bit full-on sometimes. They might ask you personal stuff.'

'I don't mind,' I said. I didn't either. I was the world's leading expert on me, and I was more than happy to share my expertise with anyone who'd listen.

'And Sean is a brat!' Leah growled.

'All younger brothers are, from what I've heard.'

'Don't go near Simba. He's not friendly.'

'Simba?'

'Our dog.'

'You never told me you had a dog,' I said. 'I love dogs!'

'Well Simba's not the lovable type, so stay away from him. He's been trained to attack strangers.'

'Any more don'ts on your list?'

There might well have been, but I never found out. The black car with tinted windows glided down Temple Street and pulled in at the kerb.

Leah opened the passenger door and said, 'Mum, this is Danni.'

Mrs Warner was slim and bird-like. Her hair was dyed black and her make-up was overdone, like a mask painted over her face. She wore a bracelet on each wrist and a ring on every finger – and her thumbs.

'Hello, Mrs Warner,' I said.

Mrs Warner stretched her mouth into a smile, but her eyes were cautious.

'Hello, Danni,' she said. 'Leah's told us all so much about you, I feel I know you already.'

That didn't stop her pumping me about hobbies, interests and school. The drive to the Grey Horse was like an exam, and Leah did nothing to take the pressure off me. She sank so far inside herself that she practically wasn't there.

When we got to the pub, I spotted a young boy playing in the car park. I twigged right away that he was Sean, because he and Leah looked alike. Sean was using a kitchen knife to hack chunks out of a wooden fence.

Mrs Warner rolled down her window and shouted, 'Stop that, Sean! How many times have you got to be told?'

Sean turned, poked out his tongue, gave his mother the finger and scampered off.

'Sorry about Sean,' Mrs Warner said to me. 'He's going through an awkward phase, you know? He'll grow out of it.'

I hoped it wouldn't take too long, because the fence looked a mess.

'Boys will be boys, won't they?' Mrs Warner said.

'Danni wouldn't know,' said Leah. 'She's an only child. She's lucky.'

As we crossed the car park, I saw a wire mesh cage behind a hedge. An animal hurled itself against the mesh, snarling savagely.

'Simba,' said Leah.

Leah needn't have bothered to warn me about not going near Simba, because walking past his cage was warning enough. He was a huge German Shepherd, with mad eyes that gazed at me like I was lunch.

Inside the pub, I met Mr Warner. He was tall and broad-shouldered, with pale blue eyes and bristly grey hair that you could see his scalp through.

'So you're Danni,' he said. 'You live on Cumberland Road, don't you?'

'Yes,' I said.

'That's on the Badger's Moon estate?'

'Yes.'

'And your father works for Thamestel Communications, right?'

'Da-ad!' said Leah, pulling me to one side. 'We're going up to my room to listen to CDs. Call us when tea's ready.'

At the foot of the stairs. I said, 'How did your dad know that?'

'What?' said Leah.

'That my dad works for Thamestel.'

'I must have told him.'

'But you've never asked me about Dad.'

Leah shrugged.

'My dad likes to check my friends out,' she said. She leaned in closer and lowered her voice to a whisper. 'Come on, I want to show you something.'

We climbed the stairs and walked along the landing. Leah paused at a door.

'This is my parents' room,' she said, still whispering. 'It's in here.'

The room smelled of perfume and air-freshener. The king-sized bed was draped with a pink satin quilt. On the wall above the headboard hung a photograph – Mr and Mrs Warner on their wedding day. Mr Warner had long brown hair and a droopy moustache; Mrs Warner was a redhead in a frothy white dress. They looked so different that it took me a few moments to recognise them.

Leah stepped over to a wardrobe, reached behind it and brought out a leather bag. She held a finger to her lips, then unzipped the bag and opened it wide enough for me to peek inside.

Light gleamed on the twin barrels of a shotgun.

I squeaked in alarm.

'Sh!' said Leah.

She rezipped the bag, put it back behind the wardrobe and we crept out on to the landing.

'What's that gun all about?' I hissed,

'Dad keeps it just in case,' Leah said.

'Just in case what?'

Leah looked me straight in the eyes.

'Werewolves,' she said.

Everything went silent. I heard the long gap between one heartbeat and the next.

'Werewolves?' I said, checking that I'd heard right.
Leah nodded.

'Werewolves are everywhere,' she said.

I searched her face, hoping that her mouth would twitch or her eyes would twinkle, anything that would let me know she was having me on.

There was nothing; Leah was serious.

9

On Saturday morning I woke up with a head full of second thoughts about Leah. I hadn't heard from her in almost six years and now suddenly she'd turned up on my doorstep and gone into a best-buddy routine. Why? We weren't the same people that we'd been in junior school. What did she want from me, exactly? I seriously considered standing her up and forgetting the whole thing, but the postman changed my mind.

The mail arrived at eight o'clock. I was having breakfast in the kitchen; Mum and Dad weren't up yet. When I heard the letter-box clatter, I went out into the hall. There was the usual selection of bills and junk mail, and a postcard addressed to me. On the front it had FLORIDA in bright pink letters, surrounded by mini-photographs of alligators, flamingos and someone dressed up as Mickey Mouse.

The message said:

AMERICA IS BRILLIANT! DISNEY WORLD
IS AMAZING! I THINK I'LL STAY
AND BE A BEACH BUM.
SEE YA!
SIMON

My insides did a roller-coaster dip and the ache came
back, just a twinge, but enough to remind me of what
I'd lost. Simon had rung me every day when we were
together; now I was just a name on his postcard list. I
didn't even rate a *wish you were here*.

My self-esteem sank like the *Titanic*, and I dived
into the only lifeboat to hand – Leah. Being myself
hadn't got me what I wanted, perhaps it was time to
be someone different. Leah had transformed herself
into a babe; if I hung out with her I might pick up a
few tips on how it was done. And besides, with my
present in such lousy shape, a stroll down Memory
Lane with someone who seemed to think that meeting
up with me again was the most exciting incident in
her life didn't seem like a bad idea. Or did it? There
was something niggling in the back of my mind – a

possible leak in the lifeboat – but I couldn't quite put my finger on what it was.

Dad came downstairs and frowned at me.

'You're not working today, are you?' he said.

'No.'

'Then why are you up so early?'

'I could ask you the same question.'

'To take your mother breakfast in bed. Give me a hand, would you, Danielle? I'm not awake enough to make tea.'

We went into the kitchen and I put the kettle on. Dad banged about in the cupboards.

'Doing anything exciting today?' he said.

'I'm going into town to meet a friend.'

'Rose?'

'No, Leah.'

Dad stopped what he was doing and looked at me, puzzled.

'You remember Leah Warner, don't you?' I said.

'Hmm.'

'She appeared out of thin air yesterday. I hardly recognised her.'

'What brought her back to Frinley?'

'Catching up with old mates. I think she wants to

show off her new image.'

'Be careful. You can't teach an old leopard new spots.'

I laughed. 'Should that have been, *you can't teach an old dog new tricks*, or, *a leopard never changes its spots*?'

'Whatever,' Dad said.

I could tell he didn't approve of my seeing Leah again, and it kind of added a little excitement to it.

It was just like old times.

Town was so hot it felt like my brains were being poached in my skull. Most of the people on the streets were wearing summery clothes, but still looked frazzled and sweaty. The air was thick and humid, and needed a thunderstorm to clear it, but the sky was relentlessly blue.

I waited just outside the entrance to the station, in the shade of the projecting roof. Eleven-thirty came and went with no sign of Leah. At eleven-forty, I began to wonder whether her train had been delayed, or she'd decided not to come.

Then I saw her, ten metres away, leaning against the safety rail near the pelican crossing. She was wearing shorts and a baggy top. There was something familar about the outfit, and I realised they were almost exactly the same clothes that I'd been wearing the day before. Her eyes were hidden behind her Ray Bans. Her smile was white.

I walked over and said, 'How long have you been standing there?'

'A couple of minutes,' said Leah. 'I wanted to look at you.'

'What for?'

'Because I like anticipation. That's the best part of being given a surprise present, isn't it? The feeling you have just before you unwrap it. It's usually better than what's inside. Where shall we go?'

'I thought we might take in the new shopping mall in Broad Street.'

Leah's jaw dropped.

'A shopping mall, in *Frinley*?' she said. 'Bring it on!'

The next hour and a half zipped by. We hit every clothes shop in the mall. Leah had a detailed knowledge of which styles were happening and which weren't, and picked out stuff that she said would suit me. I didn't take it seriously until we were both drooling over a black top in French Connection.

'You'd look really great in this, Danni,' she said.

'Agreed,' I said. 'Shame about the price tag.'

'Let me buy it for you.'

'Huh?'

'To celebrate our reunion. I can afford it. I've just been paid my monthly clothing allowance. I'll buy one too, so we can look alike.'

I had a vague recollection that Leah and I had been in this situation before, but it wouldn't come into focus.

'It's too expensive,' I said. 'Anyway, I'd never go anywhere I could wear something like that.'

Leah's eyes registered disappointment.

'I'd like to get you something,' she murmured.

I felt like a rat for bringing her down.

'Tell you what,' I said. 'Lunch is on you, OK?'

There were plenty of trendy cafés and restaurants in the mall, but as far as teenagers in Frinley were concerned, *the* place to hang on Saturday was The Web in Prospect Street. When I was little, The Web had been The Beehive, a gathering place for genteel elderly ladies. Then it had been made over as Roman Nights, a flash Italian restaurant that only survived twelve months. Its latest manifestation was a cyber-café, all stainless steel fittings, with a bank of computers against one wall. It attracted a few internet nerds, but most of the clientele went there because it served decent coffee and snacks at reasonable prices.

The Web was humming, but Leah and I managed to find a corner table. I ordered a cappuccino, and a ciabatta with melted cheese; Leah had a mineral water and a salad roll. When the food arrived, Leah ignored the roll, picking out leaves of lettuce and nibbling at them.

'So,' she said. 'Who's in the picture at the moment?'

'Which picture?'

'The boy picture.'

'Nobody,' I said. 'There's a guy at work who seems keen, but I'm not interested.'

'You've got a job?'

'At the supermarket in the Badger's Moon shopping precinct. I'm not interested in that either. How about you?'

'I don't need a job,' said Leah. She leaned across the table and lowered her voice. 'There's a boy at a table near the window. He's been staring at you ever since we came in.'

I turned and groaned.

'It's Nick,' I said.

Nick was on his own. When I caught his eye, he blushed and looked away.

Leah said, 'Is that the same Nick that you—?'

'Yeah.'

'He looks nice.'

'He is nice,' I said. 'That's his problem.'

'I don't see any problem. Let's join him.'

'What for?'

'I want to meet him.'

All the time we talked, Leah's eyes were on Nick, like the eyes of a predator sizing-up its prey. She didn't even blink as she said, 'Go on, Danni, introduce us.'

She'd paid for lunch, sweet-talked me and treated me like royalty; I didn't feel that I could say no to her.

Nick was sweet. He stood up when we stopped at his table, shook hands with Leah and the three of us sat down together. There was a moment of awkward silence and then Leah turned on the charm.

She was awesome, the most talented flirt I'd ever seen in action. She asked Nick about himself and while he replied she touched her hair, tossed her head and lowered her face so that she could look up at him through her eyelashes. When she brushed a bread crumb from the corner of his mouth, I didn't know whether to gasp or applaud.

Nick didn't stand a chance. First he was alarmed by Leah, then he was overwhelmed. The attraction that flowed between them was practically visible.

My reactions were mixed. I admired Leah's technique, but Nick's reaction gave me a pang of jealousy, as if I hadn't quite let go of him yet.

The performance came to an end when Leah said that she had a train to catch. We left a stunned Nick in The Web and went outside.

As soon as the door of the café had swung shut behind us, Leah said, 'What's Nick's surname?'

'Morrison.'

'Is he in the phone book?'

'I can give you his number if you like.'

'Ooh, yes please!'

Leah produced a pen from her shoulder bag and wrote Nick's phone number on the back of her train ticket.

'You going to call him?' I said.

'Would you mind if I did?'

'Why should I?'

'Then I might, if he's lucky.'

'You don't hold back, do you?'

'What's the point?' said Leah. 'You see some thing you want, you go for it. Life's too short to pussyfoot around.'

We said our goodbyes at the station. Neither of us mentioned meeting again, so I figured that was it: Leah had satisfied her curiosity about her childhood friend, and was going to vanish from my life the way she had before.

And what way had that been exactly? I struggled to bring it back.

10

A lot of things are still possible when you're nine. You know that fairies don't dance in a ring on your lawn at night, but you're less certain about creatures like ghosts and vampires, and evil is a power that lurks outside people, waiting to get in.

So when Leah told me that there were werewolves everywhere, I didn't know what to say, or think, or do. I silently followed her down the landing, and had my first sight of her room.

It was unbelievably neat. My bedroom was a tip, clothes and toys chucked any old where. Mum complained every once in a while, but I liked the mess because it was mine. Leah's room had been organised: a row of dolls on top of her wardrobe; a shelf of books that looked as though they'd never been opened. It was too perfect, like someone had designed a room for a girl Leah's age and moved her into it.

One thing didn't quite fit with the tweeness of the rest. The base of the bedside lamp was a wolfman, like the ones in old black-and-white horror movies, clambering over a grey rock. His fangs were bared and the torn sleeves of his shirt exposed his hairy forearms. I think it was the only genuine part of Leah in the entire room.

Leah switched on her CD-player, and the latest hit by the latest boy band pulsed out of the speakers.

'D'you like them?' Leah asked.

'You can't do that, Leah!' I said. 'You *cannot* talk about werewolves one minute and pop music the next. I want to know more.'

'Such as?'

'I thought werewolves were a made-up thing, like Santa Claus.'

'Well you were wrong.'

'Have you ever seen one?'

'Plenty of times.'

'What are they like?'

Leah chewed her bottom lip for a second, then turned down the CD-player.

'If I tell you, you mustn't tell anyone else,' she said.

'I won't.'

'Promise?'

'Promise.'

'They're not like wolves,' said Leah. 'They're not hairy with long teeth and claws, and they don't come out when the moon's full. They walk around all the time. They wear ordinary clothes and they look like ordinary people, but they're werewolves. The werewolf is inside them, where you can't see it. Once they've picked you out as a victim, they hunt you down. No matter how far you go, they follow you. They can track your scent and read your mind. If they catch you, you disappear.'

This was the most Leah had said to me in one chunk, and it took a while for me to get my head around it.

'Disappear where?' I said.

'Werewolves know places where people never go, places where no one would think of looking for you. Sometimes they turn you into one of them.'

My head spun. Leah's werewolves were changing my world, filling it with shifting shadows.

'Are there werewolves here in Frinley?' I said.

'I haven't spotted any yet, but they're bound to turn

up sooner or later.'

'But if they're so ordinary, how can you tell whether you've seen one or not?'

'Their eyes,' said Leah. 'They don't have human eyes. Their eyes are like – look, I'll show you.'

She stared at me and her yellow eyes darkened. They seemed to grow deeper and I felt myself being drawn into them.

'Stop it, Leah!' I said with a shudder. 'You're scaring me.'

Leah's eyes returned to normal.

'That's what they do,' she said. 'They look in your eyes, and you see the werewolf inside them, and you can't move.'

'They hypnotise you?'

'Yes, then they can get you to do anything they want.'

'Isn't there any protection against them?'

Leah nodded.

'Always be on watch for them,' she said. 'See them before they see you.'

'And what then?'

'Pray you can run faster than they can.'

An hour before, I'd been your regular, happy kid.

Now I didn't know what I was. I didn't think that Leah was lying to me, but if what she said was true, everything was crazy; and if it wasn't true, then Leah was the crazy one.

Mr Warner's voice came booming up the stairs, making me jump. 'Leah, Danni! Tea's ready!'

Eating with the Warners was quite an experience. Mrs Warner gave me a pub menu to choose from, then went into the kitchen to slave over a hot microwave. Mr Warner read a newspaper at the table, something my dad never did.

'Isn't Sean having tea with us?' I asked Leah.

Mr Warner answered me.

'Sean eats in his room, in front of the telly,' he said. 'He won't sit still long enough to eat a proper meal. Stuffs himself with crisps and junk food. Doesn't know he's born, that boy. When I was his age, I ate what I was given – or else!'

'Were your parents very strict with you, Mr Warner?' I said.

Mr Warner smiled.

'Nah!' he said. 'They just used to give me a clip round the ear when I didn't do as I was told.'

I ate fast. I wanted to get away from the Grey Horse

and back to the sanity of home.

As she was clearing away the dishes, Mrs Warner said, 'I'll get one of the staff to drop you home, Danni. I'd drive you myself, but I don't like taking the car out after dark.'

'Thank you,' I said, though I wasn't sure what I was thanking her for.

'You'll have to come again, Danni,' said Mr Warner. 'Drop by any time. Door's always open, in a manner of speaking.'

But then I'd have to get past Simba to reach the door, and a shotgun would be waiting on the other side.

'I'm pleased Leah's made a friend,' Mr Warner went on. 'You didn't have many at your last school, did you, Leah?'

'They thought I was a weirdo,' said Leah. 'They ganged up on me.'

'I'd better go now,' I said. 'I promised my parents that I'd be back before seven.'

Leah's shoulders sagged.

'Can't you stay longer?' she said. 'Dad can ring and say you're stopping for a bit?'

'My gran's coming over,' I said. 'She'll be

disappointed if I'm not there.'

Which was both a total lie, and the first lie I'd ever told without my face going red.

The young man who drove me home was called Terry. We didn't speak much, but when we turned into the estate, he said, 'What you make of them?'

'Who?'

'The Warners.'

'I've only just met them.'

'Funny lot,' said Terry. 'The boss has kittens every time the phone rings, and his missus dyes her hair a different colour every five minutes. And as for that dog of theirs! Puts customers off, doesn't he? Makes no sense to keep a dangerous animal like that in a pub.'

Terry was right, it didn't make sense. In fact, there were things about Leah and her family that made no sense at all.

11

Saturday evening, I went round to Rose's place for a CD-and-goss session. It was going to be our last for a fortnight because Rose was off on holiday with her family the following Monday. She insisted on the all-singing, all-dancing version of my break up with Nick, and as usual she took Nick's side.

'He must have been gutted,' she said.

I half smiled. 'I doubt it. In fact, I have a sneaking suspicion he could already be otherwise engaged.'

'Oh?'

'Guess who's back in town?'

'Who?'

I watched Rose carefully as I said, 'Leah Warner. She and I ran into Nick today. I think they've got the hots for each other.'

Rose's face went pale.

'Quite a surprise, hey?' I said.

'What does she want?'

'A rerun of the good old days.'

'There were no good old days, Danni!' said Rose. 'Leah was an emotionally disturbed weirdo. I'd have felt sorry for her if she hadn't frightened me so much.'

'You ought to see her now. We are talking cover girl. She seems to have sorted herself out big time.'

'When you say she's back, d'you mean as in permanently?' Rose asked anxiously.

'No, just a visit.'

'That's something to be thankful for. The idea of that creep hanging round the place is really freaky.'

I didn't get it. Rose could find something good to say about almost everyone, but she was acting as though Leah were as welcome as a disease.

'What happened between you two?' I said. 'You never told me all the details.'

'I never told anybody,' said Rose. 'I kind of blanked it out, you know? I can't remember if it was real or a bad dream. One thing's clear in my mind though. Leah scared the daylights out of me, and she enjoyed doing it.'

'Come on! She was only nine years old.'

Rose shuddered and wrapped her arms around herself.

'You weren't there, Danni,' she said. 'You didn't see her eyes.'

I thought, werewolf eyes.

'When she screamed at me, she sounded like an animal howling,' Rose went on. 'I never understood how you got mixed up with someone like Leah in the first place.'

I couldn't tell her. I suppose, like Rose, I'd put blanks into my memories of Leah because forgetting was easier than facing them.

I walked home. The night air wasn't exactly bracing, but it was cooler than it had been during the day. The moon was up, three-quarters full, shining its best against the background orange glare of the street lights. I was sad that Rose was going on holiday, sad about Simon, and Nick, and walking would give me a chance to think things through. Mostly, I was sad about myself.

Saturday nights with Simon had been magic – sometimes with Nick too, in an ordinary sort of way. Now I was on my own, and I wanted the special feeling back. A mild panic flashed through me: what if the special feeling had gone for ever? I'd blown it with Simon, messed up with Nick – was it because there was something wrong with me? Maybe I'd used up all my chances to be happy. I'd assumed, as you do, that Mr Right was out there some place, but there was no book of rules that said we had to meet.

Then, as I turned on to Cosham Avenue, I had an attack of *real* panic.

A figure was standing further down the street, tucked into a pocket of shadow between two lamps. It was difficult for me to be sure, but I thought it was a man wearing a parka, with the fur-lined hood pulled up to cover his face. He was so still that it was oddly threatening. Why was he hanging round an empty street on a Saturday night?

I thought, but it isn't an empty street, Danni. *You're* here.

I doubled back and ducked into an alley that would bring me out on Canfield Road, a nice, bright road that always carried a lot of traffic. I hurried down the alley, and just before I left it I looked back. The alley was as dark as a gaping mouth. Was someone hiding in the darkness?

If I'd been carrying my mobile, I would have rung Dad to come and pick me up, but my mobile was in the kitchen, plugged into its battery charger.

Chill, I thought. There's no one there.

Something moved, and my heart thumped like a pair of huge hands clapping in my chest. It might have been nothing more than a cat on the prowl, but I didn't wait to find out. I walked on as fast as I could, not wanting to surrender to my fear by running.

I knew I was safe in Canfield Road, but to get from there to home I'd have to skirt one side of Memorial Park, where there were way too many trees and bushes, and where Nick had thought we'd been watched.

Stuff went through my mind, like how the streets weren't safe at night, and how lone females were prime victims. The closer I got to Memorial Park, the wilder my thoughts became. Childhood nightmares came out of hiding and danced in the shadows: the monster under the bed; the vampire in his bats' wings cloak; all the creatures I could laugh at in the daytime.

The park was dead ahead, opposite Memorial Hall and the war memorial, a floodlit stone pillar carved with lists of names. I glanced over my shoulder.

Someone was behind me, too far away for me to see clearly, but close enough to keep me in sight.

That did it. I broke into a run. Previously, the highlight of my athletics career had been taking part in the finals of a relay race on Sports Day when I was in Year Eight. That night I outdid myself, only there was no crowd to cheer me on, just rows of silent houses. Danni the Control Freak had been transformed into a terrified little girl.

My adrenalin stopped pumping at the end of my street. I halted to catch my breath and looked back. There was no one in sight. I'd lost whoever had been following me, if anyone *had* been following me. I walked the rest of the way, feeling that I'd overreacted. My imagination had gone haywire when David took my photograph, and now it had happened again. I'd seen a totally innocent guy waiting for someone on Cosham Avenue, and jumped to all the wrong conclusions.

When I got in, Mum took one look at me and said, 'Have you been running?'

'Yeah,' I said. 'I didn't want to miss my curfew.'

Mum frowned.

'But you've still got twenty minutes to go,' she said.

I shrugged. 'Watch must be wrong.'

I didn't tell her that I'd panicked because I thought I was being tailed. Acting like a jerk isn't something you want to share with anyone, is it?

But some good had come out of it. Running past Memorial Park had jogged my memory, and a lot of missing pieces had fallen into place.

12

After my visit to the Grey Horse, Leah opened up to me. We spent breaktimes and lunch-times together, and I waited with her after school until her mum came to drive her home. Leah told me all she knew about werewolves, and I was gradually drawn into her world. Werewolves, she said, had invented legends about themselves to fool people into thinking that they didn't exist. Governments kept quiet about them because they didn't want to cause a massive panic, and because some werewolves were rich and powerful enough to buy their silence. She went into such convincing detail that it didn't seem possible she could be making it up, and she showed me evidence. According to Leah, the strange scratches in the tarmac at one corner of the playground had been made by a werewolf sharpening its claws. A mark on the concrete paving outside the school kitchen was an old bloodstain. I didn't want to believe any of these things, but challenging Leah would have been like rejecting her friendship, and I was anxious not to hurt her feelings. I'd had friends before, people I'd played skipping and ball games with during break, but I'd never been as close to anyone as I was to Leah. She shared her innermost secrets with me, and I felt privileged.

After a fortnight of Leah's stories, I had the worst nightmare of my life. I was lost in a moonlit forest, standing at the edge of a swamp, with a werewolf close behind me. Unable to go forward or back, I stood listening to the werewolf's panting breath and scuffling claws drawing closer and closer. If I turned my head I'd see it, but I was paralysed with fear...

I woke. My pillow was damp with sweat. A car passed in the street outside and the twin beam of its headlights made shadows move around the bedroom walls. I lay shivering. The only way I could calm myself was to imagine that I was inside a transparent bubble, fitted with revolving machine-guns that pumped out streams of silver bullets. That's when I realised something that my nine-year-old self couldn't have put into words. I'd reached the point where Leah's fantasies had the strength of reality. She'd surrounded me with a thicket of stories, and if I didn't break free she was going to consume me, devour my personality so that I wouldn't have any will or identity of my own.

I pinned my hopes on the Christmas holidays. During the last two weeks of term, Leah didn't mention anything about the two of us meeting up over the holidays, and I decided that I wouldn't mention it either. Being home with Mum and Dad would be a welcome relief.

No such luck. The day after term ended, I went shopping with Mum. We had lunch in a pizza joint, and while we were eating, Mum said, 'Will you be seeing Leah over Christmas?'

'I don't think so,' I said. 'She's pretty busy with her family.'

'Her parents must be busy too. I don't envy them, running a pub at this time of year. Why don't you invite Leah over for a meal? It would be a nice gesture, and her parents might be glad to get her out from under their feet.'

'I'm not sure, Mum,' I gabbled. 'Leah doesn't go out

much. Her parents are very protective, and—'

Mum frowned at me suspiciously.

'Have you and Leah had an argument?' she said.

'No, only...'

'Only what?'

I wanted to tell Mum the truth. I wanted to say, 'Leah believes in werewolves, her parents keep a shotgun in their bedroom, her brother's a delinquent and the family pet is a man-eating dog.' But I'd promised Leah that I'd never tell anyone.

'Nothing,' I said. 'I'll give her a call later.'

'You don't seem terribly enthusiastic. Are you sure you haven't fallen out with Leah?'

'Certain,' I said. 'We're fine.'

I phoned the Grey Horse at six, and offered Leah the invitation. I was expecting her to make an excuse like she usually did, but instead she said, 'Can I?'

'That's why I rang,' I said.

'Great! Hang on, I'll ask Mum.'

The phone rattled as Leah put her hand over the mouthpiece. I heard muffled voices, then Mrs Warner came on the line.

'It's ever so kind of you to invite her,' she said. 'Are

you sure it won't be too much trouble?'

'No trouble at all.'

'I know this is a cheek, but you couldn't make it this Friday, could you? We have to go to London, and Leah isn't that keen on coming with us. If we drop her over at five and pick her up at nine, will that be all right?'

'I'll check,' I said.

I found Mum, talked to her and then went back to the phone.

'Friday's OK,' I said, 'but Mum says you don't have to pick Leah up. Dad will give her a lift to the pub.'

'I'm afraid that's not convenient,' said Mrs Warner. 'Greg – Leah's father – will want to drive her himself. He doesn't like Leah accepting lifts from strangers. He worries about accidents.'

I felt offended on Dad's behalf.

'My father's a really careful driver, Mrs Warner,' I said.

'Oh, I'm sure he is! But better to be safe than sorry, eh?'

Mrs Warner handed the phone back to Leah. Leah was excited, and it made me feel guilty. The truth was that asking her over to my house was like opening the front door and inviting the werewolves inside.

The following Friday, Leah turned up at five o' clock on the dot, carrying a huge bouquet for Mum. The flowers were bright pink, purple and orange, and you could hear the colours clashing.

'You shouldn't have,' Mum said.

'No problem,' said Leah.

'Take Leah into the lounge, Danni. I'll just go and pop these in some water.'

Mum sounded as if she'd really like to pop the flowers into a bin.

In the lounge, Leah stood in the middle of the carpet, looking round.

'Grab a chair,' I said. 'Are you all right? You look tired.'

She looked worse than tired; she was even paler than normal and there were dark rings under her eyes.

Leah flopped.

'I hate Christmas!' she grunted. 'Rushing around, buying presents and putting up decorations – why do people bother?'

'It's a family thing,' I said.

Leah wrinkled her nose.

'Don't talk to me about families!' she said. 'Sean's being a bigger pain than ever. He's nagging Mum and Dad to get him a Playstation and one of those light-guns so he can play shoot-'em-ups. What are your parents giving you?'

'I don't know.'

'I'll get money, like I always do. Dad asked me to make a list of things I wanted, but I couldn't be bothered.'

'Have your parents gone shopping in London?'

'They're hunting werewolves,' Leah said.

The temperature in the room took a sharp drop.

As gently as I could, I said, 'Leah, I don't think you should mention werewolves in front of my mum and dad. They wouldn't understand.'

'You don't believe me, do you?'

It was the straight question that I'd been dreading.

'I'll show you a werewolf one day,' Leah went on, 'and then you'll know.'

I kept quiet, because I couldn't think of a reply.

Leah was two people that evening, moody and sullen when we were alone together, bright and cheerful when my parents were around. During tea, she kept up a stream of chatter that astonished me because it was so unlike the Leah I knew.

When Mum asked a polite question about her parents, Leah said, 'Dad used to run a night-club in London before he was a pub manager. That's how he met Mum. She was a singer. She signed a recording contract once, but the company got taken over and the new owners did the dirty on her, so she never made a record. She knows some quite famous people in the business.'

I saw my parents exchange glances.

Dad said, 'And what do you all think of Frinley, now that you've settled in?'

'It's OK,' said Leah, 'but I miss my horse. We had to sell him before we moved. I think my kid brother Sean is missing his friends.'

'He'll soon make new ones,' Mum said.

'He won't find that easy,' said Leah. 'He's very highly strung. He's going to be excluded from school.'

'I beg your pardon?'

'It's not his fault. This bully kept picking on him, and Sean got into a fight. The headmaster says that Sean pulled a knife, but Sean would never take a knife to school. The bully must have planted it on him, to get him into trouble.'

'That's dreadful!' said Mum.

Leah smiled.

'Sean's not bothered,' she said. 'It's always happening. He's used to it by now. Sean's too trusting for his own good.'

She went on and on, inventing the family that she wished she had – a sensitive brother, a kind father and a talented mother who'd given up a promising career to raise children. I didn't know how much was fact and how much was fiction, and I don't think that Leah knew either.

Somehow we struggled through until nine, when Mr Warner turned up to collect Leah. Even though it was dark, he wore sunglasses, and he turned down Mum's offer of a drink.

'Can't stay,' he said. 'Sorry about the shades, migraine coming on. Did Leah behave herself?'

'Yes,' said Mum.

'Glad to hear it.' Mr Warner turned to Leah, and the lenses of his sunglasses flashed. 'Come on, trouble! I'm grateful for your hospitality, Mrs Vance. I'm sure Leah appreciated it.'

After Mr Warner and Leah left, Mum and Dad

disappeared into the kitchen for a long time. Eventually Dad came into the lounge and sat next to me on the sofa.

'Your friend Leah has a lively imagination, hasn't she?' he said.

'She gets carried away sometimes.'

Dad wriggled and cleared his throat awkwardly.

'I shouldn't get too involved with Leah if I were you,' he said, 'and don't encourage her to tell those stories of hers. That kind of thing can be unhealthy if it gets out of hand.'

It was good advice, and I'd come to much the same conclusion myself, but it was already too late.

13

My imagination might have been working overtime on Saturday night but on Monday, after I'd finished at the supermarket, I was definitely followed – or encountered at least. As I was walking through the precinct, I saw Nick standing near the entrance to Iceland. He quickly turned around and stared at the window, doing the worst impression of not noticing me that I'd ever seen.

I went over and tapped him on the shoulder.

'Hi,' I said. 'Thinking of buying a freezer?'

Nick's face glowed red. Apart from the blush, he was looking good. His hair was carefully tousled and he had on a pair of those blue-lensed shades that Australian cricketers wear.

'Oh, hi, Danni,' he said. 'Fancy bumping into you.'

'I'm working in the supermarket, Nick. You know

what time my shift finishes, so there's nothing fancy about it. Were you waiting for me?'

Nick's shoulders sagged.

'Um, kind of,' he mumbled.

'Why?'

'Er, the friendship thing,' said Nick. 'Remember you said you wanted us to stay friends? I want us to stay friends too.'

'But you told me that we'd never been friends,' I pointed out.

'I changed my mind. Want to hang out for a while?'

Nick was lying; he hadn't lied to me before and I didn't know what to make of it.

'I'm on my way home,' I said. 'I was up at half six and I'm shattered.'

'Mind if I walk part of the way with you?'

We strolled down Woodfield Road. The air was heavy, and the heat shimmer made the brick walls wobble like jelly.

Nick seemed on edge, his eyes flicking this way and that as if he were searching for somebody.

'Heard from Leah?' I said.

'Uh-huh. We went out together on Saturday night.'

I felt a twinge. It wasn't envy, more like a feeling

that Nick had let me down. I knew I had no right to feel that way, so I ignored it and said, 'How was it?'

Nick frowned.

'Kind of weird,' he said. 'We went to a movie, and while we were waiting in the ticket queue, all she did was talk about you. She asked about our first date – where we went, what you wore, what you said and, er...' Nick's voice tailed off.

'And?'

'The minute the lights went down, she jumped me. She didn't so much kiss me as try to eat my face. Afterwards, she asked if she kissed the same way you did.'

'You're kidding!'

'No I'm not. Neither was Leah. She's fascinated by you. I think you're sort of her big hero, you know?'

'Heroine,' I said. 'She must have been winding you up, Nick.'

'Maybe.'

'Feel free to pick my brains about Leah. That is why you arranged to meet me accidentally on purpose, isn't it?'

'I'm not that interested in Leah. To tell you the truth, she was way too full-on for me.'

'Then why are you—?'

Nick said, 'For what it's worth, I miss you.'

He was being honest, and at that moment I missed him too, though I wasn't about to admit it, but I sensed that there was something else.

'You're holding out on me,' I said. 'Give me a break and be straight, will you, Nick?'

Nick coughed nervously and ran his hand through his hair.

'OK, straight,' he said. 'Rose is worried about you. She rang me yesterday and told me about the calls you've been getting. She wanted me to check on you while she's away, make sure you're not hassled by some perv.'

There are days when your paranoia is bang to rights – my best mate and my ex had been hatching little schemes behind my back. They'd only done it because they cared about me, but I was in no mood to be appreciative. The panic attack I'd suffered on the way home from Rose's on Saturday night had shaken me more badly than I realised, and I lashed out.

'It's none of your business, Nick!' I snapped. 'I'm not your girlfriend any more and I don't need a bodyguard, thanks. What were you expecting, that I'd swoon into your big, manly arms?'

'I gave up expecting anything from you a long time ago,' said Nick. 'I'm just doing what Rose asked me to do.'

I thought I had it worked out. This was something Rose had dreamed up to try and get me and Nick together again.

'Well I'm asking you not to,' I said. 'Get off my case.'

Nick pushed his shades up on to his forehead, looked me in the eyes and said, 'Hey, it's me, Danni.'

And it was: the Nick who'd bent over backwards to keep me happy; the Nick I'd given the runaround; the Nick I'd used as ointment when Simon bruised my pride. I hadn't gone out with him, I'd exploited him. The shame and anger were too much to handle.

'Leave me alone, Nick,' I said, and stomped off. I regretted it almost immediately, but I was too confused and stubborn to go back and apologise.

By the time I reached home, my anger had shifted focus. Where did Rose get off, sneaking around and playing Cupid? If she hadn't been on holiday, I would have rung her and given her a rollicking. It was like she thought she knew what was good for me better than I knew it myself. How could she do that, after all we'd been through?

Then I started to go over all that Rose and I *had* been through: more memories, more pieces slotting together.

14

That Christmas, Thamestel abandoned the usual Christmas party for the families of its employees and paid for a coach load of kids and parents to go to the matinée of a West End show. I went because Mum and Dad were going and I wasn't looking forward to it very much, but it turned out OK in the end because I met Rose.

I clocked her as soon as I climbed on the bus. I'd seen her around school and I knew she was in my year, but she was in a different class and I'd never spoken to her. Rose was skinny, with straight fair hair and a quirky face, like a pixie's. She noticed me get on the bus and half-smiled to show that she recognised me. I half-smiled back and sat down with my parents.

Traffic in London was a nightmare. The coach pulled up outside the theatre with minutes to spare and everybody charged off like invading soldiers. We were just about seated when the houselights dimmed.

The show was a musical – terminally naff, but with great costumes and some spectacular special effects. During the interval I joined the queue for the Ladies and found myself standing next to Rose.

She smiled shyly at me and said, 'Is it just me, or is this show boring?'

'It's definitely not just you,' I said, smiling back.

'Your parents make you come?'

I nodded.

'Mine too,' said Rose. 'I tried to get out of it, but my dad said I had to. I'm Rose, by the way.'

'Danni,' I said.

'You're in Miss Penhaligan's class, aren't you? Don't you hang out with that girl, what's her name – Lynne?'

'Leah,' I said.

Rose pulled a face.

'Some of the girls in school say nasty things about her.'

'What sort of things?'

'They call her Wolfie because she growls and snaps at everybody.'

I remembered Leah's werewolf eyes, and *Wolfie* was so perfect that I laughed.

'She doesn't snap at me – much,' I said.

For the next ten minutes I giggled, goofed and generally behaved like a going-on ten-year-old. Rose was fun in exactly the same way that Leah wasn't. At the end of the interval we went back to our parents, but on the coach ride home Rose and I sat next to each other.

When the coach reached the outskirts of Frinley, Rose glanced out of the window and said, 'Oh! Are we there already?' She looked really disappointed. Then she turned to me. 'Would you like to meet up again some time over the holiday, Danni?'

'I'd love to!' I said.

We swapped phone numbers, and that was it – instant mates.

The buzz I had from meeting Rose lasted until Dad opened the front door and said, 'What's this?'

He picked up an envelope from the doormat and turned it over.

'It's for you, Danni,' he said.

I took the envelope and opened it. Inside was a card from Leah – *Happy Christmas to a Dear Friend* – and a locket and chain. The locket had two clasped hands engraved on it.

'Can I have a look?' said Mum.

She examined the locket under the hall light.

'You can't accept this, Danni,' she said.

'Why not?' I said.

'It's real gold – see the hallmarks? You'll have to give it back.'

Mum was right, and Leah wasn't going to be pleased.

I phoned Leah on Christmas morning.

'Did you like your surprise?' she said.

'Um—' I said.

'I asked Mum and Dad to get it when they were in London. It's an antique. The two hands on the locket stand for eternal friendship.'

'Leah,' I said, 'my mum won't let me take it. She says it's too much.'

'No it isn't! I want you to have it.'

I tried joking my way out of the awkwardness.

'What did you have to go and spend all that money for?' I said. 'Couldn't you have got me a sparkly hairband or something?'

'You don't like it,' Leah said in a quiet, disappointed voice.

'It's not that I don't like it, it's my mum. She says I have to return it to you.'

'Can't you hide it and wear it secretly so only we know?'

'No,' I said. 'I promised.'

'Bring it round tomorrow. You can stay to lunch and—'

'I'm busy tomorrow. We're going to see my grandparents. Sorry.'

Leah's tone hardened to tough-little-cookie.

'No problem,' she said. 'Post the locket back to me, it doesn't matter.'

'Don't get humpty.'

'Who's humpty? It's only a lousy locket.'

'It was a nice thought,' I said. 'Especially when I didn't get you anything.'

'You've given me loads,' said Leah. 'The present was a way of saying thank you.'

Just for a moment I glimpsed the real Leah – a big, clumsy girl with no real friends. Something told me that I wasn't the first person she'd tried to buy.

'Have to go now,' I said. 'I'm helping Mum get

lunch ready.'

'See you soon?'

'Sure,' I said, lying.

The weekend after Christmas, Rose and I went shopping, armed with vouchers and gift-money. We did what girls our age were supposed to do: we checked out the latest film tie-in merchandising in the Warner Brothers shop, drooled over expensive boxes of chocolates and had giggling fits over stupid things that no one else would have found funny. We were alike in many ways, but different enough to find each other interesting.

'D'you believe in creepy stuff, like magic and witches?' I said while we were having lunch in a burger bar.

'I do when I'm watching it on TV or in a movie, but not afterwards,' said Rose, stirring her milkshake with a straw. 'I was afraid of vampires when I was little, but my mum proved to me that they couldn't exist,' she said.

'How?'

'With a calculator.'

'Huh?'

'If a vampire bites someone, they become a vampire too,' Rose explained. 'So the first night you have two vampires, next night you have four and the next you have sixteen. After seven nights, the calculator went on to overload. So the entire population of the world would be vampires in a week, and d'you see any?'

'How about werewolves?' I asked as casually as possible.

'I don't believe in monsters,' said Rose.

'And ghosts?'

'I'm more interested in life before death. Being nine is a pain, isn't it? You're too young to do the things you really want to do, and eventually you turn into a moody teenager, like my big sis. She spends most of her time on the phone.'

Rose gave me a rundown of her sister's love life, which was incredibly complicated.

We had such a great time together that we arranged to meet the next day.

I set off for home, certain that I'd found a genuine friend at last, and determined to cut my ties with Leah; but it wasn't going to be as easy as that.

15

Thursday morning, the supermarket was busy. Thursday being pension day, droves of pensioners turned up to do their weekly shopping. Many of them needed help because the supermarket was running an organic food promotion and a lot of items had been relocated to make room for it. I found it quicker to take the customers to what they wanted rather than get involved in giving complicated directions. Some of the other staff found the pensioners irritating, but I didn't mind, though it was a bit like being a tourist guide.

Towards the end of my shift I was taken off shelf-stacking and sent to the checkouts to lend a hand with packing so that the customers went through faster. Standing proved to be tougher than walking around: I'd been rushed off my feet all morning and my feet were starting to complain. A foot sauna and a deep massage with peppermint foot-lotion were definitely in order. I was planning a slobby afternoon, watching daytime TV.

It didn't work out that way.

I heard a tapping on the window behind me, turned, and there was Leah standing outside. She blew me a showbiz kiss – MWAH! – and raised her hand to show me her wrist watch. I flashed the fingers and thumbs of both hands to indicate ten minutes. Leah nodded.

She seemed delighted to see me, and I remembered what Nick had said about my being her hero. I thought that anyone who regarded me as a hero figure had to have a pretty sad kind of life, but I was touched nevertheless.

When we eventually met up, Leah hugged me and said, 'You look terrific!'

'No I don't,' I said. 'I look sweaty and knackered. You're the terrific-looking one.'

'Can you spare me some time? I can only stay an hour or so. I have to be in London by four, but I had to grab the chance to see you again.'

'I'm glad you did,' I said. 'My social life is on hold

at the moment, and Rose went to Greece with her family yesterday.'

'So, you're all mine,' Leah murmured.

I laughed, but thought, that's a strange way of putting it.

'Is there anywhere we can get a drink?' said Leah. 'I'm gagging.'

We went to the precinct café. I had an OJ, Leah stuck to mineral water.

'I hear you dated Nick on Saturday night,' I said.

'D'you mind?'

'No, but did you really ask him about how I snog?'

'Did he tell you that?'

'Uh-huh.'

'Boys and their dreams! I just asked him how you met, to make conversation. He must have got the wrong end of the stick.'

I took a menu from the table and used it as a fan. My face was streaming, but Leah hadn't even broken sweat.

'How d'you manage to stay so cool?' I said. 'The heat's killing me.'

Leah swirled her glass around so that the ice cubes in it tinkled.

'I learned how to cope with heat in Spain,' she said.

'Anyway, this isn't so hot. It's the humidity that's getting to you. In Spain, the heat's drier. Mum and Dad have a big apartment, with a balcony that overlooks a little harbour. Dad's probably taking a siesta there right now, sunning himself and swigging a big gin and tonic.'

'And you'd rather be *here*?'

Leah shrugged with one shoulder.

'It's boring where my parents live,' she said. 'Most of the people in the village are ex-pat Brits, all middle-aged or older. They go to Dad's bar and watch football on TV – how pathetic is that?'

'Why did your folks move to Spain?'

Leah's mouth twitched at one corner.

'Oh, you know, business stuff,' she said. 'One of Dad's mates offered him a lease on the bar and Dad went for it.'

Leah was obviously uncomfortable about discussing her parents, so I changed the subject.

'What's boarding school like?' I said.

'Like a prison, with no time off for good behaviour.'

'Have you made loads of friends there?'

Leah paused for a moment, then said, 'Not real friends. Not friends like we were.'

It began to dawn on me that she'd idealised our friendship, built it up to be something that it hadn't actually been. She'd done the same to me, put me on a pedestal.

'I wasn't that good a friend,' I said.

Leah either didn't hear me or chose to ignore my comment.

'D'you think the supermarket would give me a job?' she said.

'I thought you didn't need one.'

'I don't, but it would be fun to work together, wouldn't it? We'd get to see more of each other.'

I wasn't so sure that I wanted to see more of Leah and tried to think of a tactful reply, but I didn't need to come up with one, because Leah switched her attention elsewhere. She stared over my left shoulder, and there was a hungry expression on her face.

'Hmm!' she said throatily. 'Check out the eye candy.'

David was sitting two tables away from us with his face buried in a book, chewing a sandwich. His camera was next to the plate in front of him.

'His name's David,' I said. 'He works in the

supermarket too. He's into photography.'

Outrageous Leah came out to play. She stood up, marched over to David and said, 'Hello, David who works in the same supermarket as Danni. Want to take a picture of us?'

She charmed him, just like she'd charmed Nick in The Web, and David couldn't resist. He must have found the whole thing as embarrassing as I did, but if Leah noticed our embarrassment, she ignored it.

Before I knew it, David was snapping away while Leah and I posed, though it was Leah who did most of the posing. She pouted, cocked her hip, flung her arms around me, stretched her mouth into a film-premier grin; she was coy Leah, flirty Leah, Leah the star.

Finally, David said, 'That's it. No more memory on the smart card.'

Leah pestered him to show her the pictures on the tiny monitor on the back of the camera.

'I want copies of all of them,' she said. 'When will they be ready? How much will they cost?'

'No charge. I'll print them tonight and give them to Danni tomorrow,' said David. 'Unless you'd like to pick them up yourself.'

Leah went coy.

'Is that an invitation?' she said.

'Could be.'

'I'll have to take a rain-check. I'm going to visit relatives in London for a couple of days. In fact, I'd better make tracks right now. Where's the nearest bus stop, Danni?'

'I'll walk you there,' I said. 'It's on my way.'

When we were safely out of David's earshot, I said, 'I can't believe what you just did! You're shameless.'

'He fancies you,' said Leah.

'Yeah? Not as much as he fancies you.'

'He fancies us both. We could tie him in knots, no problem.'

Something about the way Leah said it made me ask, 'Is that what you do to guys, get them wrapped around your little finger?'

'Only the soppy ones – you know, the guys who come on deep and meaningful? They're begging for it.'

Her voice was hard; I glimpsed the cruel streak that ran below her surface and was grateful that I wasn't on the receiving end.

The bus stop was up ahead. A man was standing at

it with his back turned. One thing about him struck me as peculiar: even though it was boiling hot, he was wearing a brown raincoat. Leah saw him and froze. She grabbed my arm, pulled me into the nearest front garden and half-crouched behind a hedge.

'Leah, what are you doing?' I said.

She was breathing quickly, almost hyperventilating.

'That man at the bus stop,' she panted.

'What about him?'

'I don't want him to see me.'

'Why not?'

'I haven't got time to explain. See if he's still there, will you, Danni?'

I stepped out on to the pavement. The man was consulting the timetable that was attached to the bus stop sign, shifting his weight from foot to foot like he had to keep an important appointment and was anxious that he might be late.

'Still there,' I said softly.

When Leah didn't respond, I went back into the front garden and she'd gone. She'd slipped away so stealthily that I hadn't seen or heard her. It reminded me of how good she was at disappearing.

For the rest of the afternoon, I thought about Leah.

Maybe it wasn't just coincidence that she'd reappeared in my life. Something was going on, something that she hadn't told me about, and I was determined to find out what.

16

Over that Christmas holiday, my friendship with Rose grew firmer. I could be completely honest with her in a way I hadn't been able to with anyone else, and she could turn a problem into laughter faster than anybody I'd ever known.

One afternoon we went to the movies, and as we were walking across the cinema car park, I saw a young boy running along a row of parked cars, flipping wing mirrors and aerials; a woman was yelling at him. The woman was Mrs Warner and the boy was Sean.

'Oh no!' I groaned.

'What's the matter?' said Rose.

'Can we go around to the side door?'

Before Rose could answer, Mrs Warner spotted me and waved.

'Coo-ee! Danni!'

She tottered over on her high heels. She was wearing sunglasses and a head scarf. The line of hair that showed under the scarf was an unconvincing shade of auburn. Her skin was fake-tan orange.

'Fancy meeting you here!' she said.

I mumbled something about the movie that Rose and I were going to.

'You're quite a stranger these days,' Mrs Warner said.

'I've been busy,' I said. 'You know what Christmas is like.'

'Leah's starting to worry that she must have done something to offend you.'

'It's nothing like that.'

'I'm sure she'd appreciate a visit, though she's too stubborn to ring you up and ask you. You know how stubborn she is.' Mrs Warner nodded her head at Rose. 'Is this a friend of yours?'

'Yes,' I said. 'Rose, this is Mrs Warner, Leah's mother.'

'Why don't the both of you come over?' said Mrs Warner. 'Leah would like that.'

I sincerely doubted it.

I said, 'You'll have to excuse us, Mrs Warner. The

movie starts soon.'

'Don't let me keep you but remember, you're welcome any time,' Mrs Warner said. She turned and shouted, 'Sean, leave those cars alone or there'll be no telly for a week!'

Rose and I carried on towards the cinema.

'That's Leah's mother?' said Rose. 'No wonder the girl's weird! And who was that kid?'

'Sean, Leah's brother.'

'They ought to keep him on a lead. Are you really going to their place?'

'Not if I can help it,' I said. 'Leah wants me to be her best friend but...'

'But what?'

Explaining took such a long time that I had to break off for the movie. I finished the story afterwards, in the cinema foyer, drinking watery cola.

'Werewolves?' said Rose. 'You're kidding!'

'I wish.'

'And Leah wasn't kidding?'

'Definitely not.'

Rose whistled.

'She should see a doctor – she's mad!' she said.

'I don't know what to do,' I said. 'I feel sorry for

Leah because she's lonely, but the things she talks about are kind of creepy, you know?'

'And creepy isn't a good way to feel about a friend, is it? I'd drop her if I were you.'

'How?'

Rose shrugged.

'Easy,' she said. 'When Leah's about, be somewhere else. She'll get the message.'

'Yeah, but how long will it take?'

And more importantly, what would Leah's reaction be?

I went over it and over it in my mind, searching for a compromise. I imagined Rose, Leah and me together, and it just wouldn't work. Rose and Leah were opposites: Rose was bright, open and funny; Leah was dark, secretive and moody. They wouldn't hit it off in a million years. Leah was too demanding to be willing to share me, but somehow she was going to have to learn.

First day back at school it snowed, which made a mockery of its being the first day of spring term. The flakes fell thinly, appearing and disappearing before you could see them properly. Gusts of wind played with the snow, twisting it into whirlpools.

As I walked up Temple Road, I saw Leah standing at the main gate and I knew that she was waiting for me. I approached her with my widest false grin.

'Hi!' I said. 'It's freezing, isn't it?'

'I don't mind the cold,' said Leah.

'Have a good Christmas?'

'No. Dad got drunk and had a row with Mum. Sean gave everybody grief. I spent most of the time on my own in my bedroom.'

Leah didn't add, 'And you never bothered to come and see me,' but it was hanging in the air between us.

'That must have been boring,' I said.

'Tell me about it. At least I was safe from the werewolves, but I knew they were there. I woke up in the middle of the night and heard them moving around outside.'

'Are you sure it wasn't Simba?'

Leah gave me a what-would-you-know look.

'I can tell the difference between a dog and a werewolf,' she said. 'I thought we might have got away from them this time, but we haven't. I should've known better.'

I was confused – was the despair in Leah's voice

genuine, or was she putting it on to get my sympathy?

'Leah,' I said, 'have you ever thought that the werewolves might only be in your head?'

Leah smiled a strange smile, and I noticed how the tips of her long canine teeth touched her bottom lip. Then the smile shrank as she caught sight of someone coming up behind us. I turned and saw Rose.

Rose said, 'Have you seen my bottom anywhere? I had it first thing, but I think it's frozen off.'

I laughed, and introduced her to Leah.

Leah was wary, said, 'Hi,' and then lapsed into silence. Rose and I chatted, and I kept trying to include Leah in the conversation. All I could get out of her was the occasional grunt, but she watched Rose closely with an unblinking stare.

The registration bell rang. Rose headed for her form room, Leah and I went off in the opposite direction.

'Rose is nice, isn't she?' I said.

'Rose Palmer,' said Leah, 'Fifty-Eight, Wessex Close. Her father's an electronic engineer with Thamestel, her mother works part time at Manor Field Primary. Her sister Catherine goes to Pound Lane Comp.'

'What is this, Leah? How did you—'

I broke off as I remembered how much her father had known about me. Mr Warner had obviously had his spies out.

'You've been checking up on Rose, haven't you?' I said. 'Your mother told you that she'd seen us together, and you went snooping. Why?'

'You don't understand, Danni. When you live the way I do, you can't trust anybody. It pays to find out about people.'

'And what way would that be? How *do* you live exactly?'

'In fear,' Leah said.

I didn't need to ask her what she was afraid of.

For the rest of the week Leah didn't talk to me much. I took this as a good sign, and hoped it meant that our friendship was crumbling, but then I noticed that every once in a while Leah would get a smug look in her eyes and smirk to herself, and I knew that she was up to something.

I found out what Leah was up to on Friday morning. She was absent from school, which was a relief at first, but I didn't stay relieved for long, because at breaktime Rose found me.

Rose was pale and all the laughter had gone from her eyes.

'You OK?' I said.

'No,' said Rose. 'Leah was at the corner of my street when I left for school this morning. She threatened me.'

'She *what*?'

'She said that you were her friend, she'd found you first, and that she'd beat me up if I didn't leave you alone. It was really scary, Danni!'

I wished that I could have told Rose that Leah was all talk, but I'd seen Leah handle Becky Tillotson, and I knew how violent she could be.

'She's just jealous,' I said. 'You should report her to the Head. She's trying to frighten you.'

'And it's working,' said Rose. 'If I tell the Head, Leah might get even more annoyed with me.'

Rose looked so worried and vulnerable that it made a wave of cold anger wash over me.

'Leah's off today,' I said, 'but I'm going round to see her straight after school. She needs putting right about a few things.'

'Don't, Danni! I wouldn't want you to get into a fight because of me.'

'This isn't about you, it's about me and Leah,' I said.

I could see it all. Leah wanted to be in control; she wanted to take over my life and turn me into her pet – and I wasn't about to let her.

17

David showed me the photographs he'd taken of me and Leah during my morning break on Friday. They weren't the best photographs of myself that I'd ever seen; I looked stiff and awkward, like I'd rather be some place else.

'That friend of yours is really something,' said David. 'What was her name again?'

'Leah,' I told him.

'Are you two related?'

'No, why?'

'You look vaguely alike. I thought you might be cousins or something.'

I examined the photographs more closely. I'd never thought of Leah and me as being alike in any way, but now that David mentioned it, I could see what he meant. We were roughly the same height and weight, and in one or two pictures Leah had copied my stance, my facial expression and the sullen glint in my eyes. We were echoes of each other.

'Does she live round here?' said David.

'No. Her family moved to Spain. She's on holiday.'

'When is she going back?'

'She hasn't said.'

David adjusted his spectacles, pulled at his collar and said, 'Have you got her address or phone number? I'd like to photograph her again before she leaves.'

'Sorry,' I said. 'I have no idea where she's staying or what her number is.'

It wasn't until I'd said it out loud that I realised how one-sided this was. Leah could contact me but I couldn't contact her – strange way to run a friendship.

David didn't believe me.

'OK, be like that,' he said sourly.

'I'm not holding out on you, David. I honestly don't know. I'll ask her next time I see her, but I warn you, she's a bit of a man-eater.'

'Is that right?' David said with a grin.

I'd meant to put him off, but instead I'd sharpened his interest.

Nothing about Leah was straightforward, not even

the effect she had on males. Questions about her didn't get answered, but led to more questions. Such as: why hadn't she given me her number or address; who was she hiding from; and top of the list was the question that Rose had asked – what did Leah want?

It occurred to me that I might not see her again after her vanishing act the day before. If she'd gone to London, like she'd said she was going to, there were more hiding-places available than there were in Frinley, if hiding places were what she was after. She might even be back in Spain, lying in the sun on her parents' balcony. To be honest, I wished that she *was* there, so I could get back to normal, carry on with my life and stop remembering things that made me freak.

The heat was draining, and everybody at work talked about it. Someone said the weather was due to break at the weekend, and as I walked home I searched the sky, hoping to see clouds, but there weren't any. Melted tar glistened on the roads and the tyres of passing cars hissed as if they were driving through rain. The air smelled of exhaust fumes, sweet and dusty. I was thirsty, tired and so brain-dead I could hardly think straight.

Then, as I was walking up the front path, someone came around the side of the house and gave me a jolt of adrenalin that went through me like needles.

It was Leah, though it took me a few seconds to recognise her. The glamour-puss had gone, and she was dressed like any other kid our age: loose sweatshirt with long sleeves that covered her hands, baggy jeans, scuzzy trainers, hair tucked inside a baseball cap whose peak was pulled down over her face.

I said, 'Leah! You nearly frightened the life out of me.'

'I didn't mean to,' said Leah. 'I got here an hour ago. I waited in the back garden so no one would see me.'

'Why aren't you in London?'

Leah stepped closer. Her eyes were big and haunted; tears brimmed over her bottom lids.

'I'm in trouble, Danni,' she whispered. 'Big trouble.'

A dark shadow from the past fell across me and I felt a sudden chill of fear.

'You'd better come inside,' I said.

We went into the lounge. Leah took the armchair that was furthest away from the window, drew her feet up under her and practically tucked herself into a ball.

'Has this got anything to do with that guy at the

bus stop yesterday?'

Leah nodded.

I said, 'Are you going to tell me about it, or are we going to play guessing games?'

'Can I ask you something first?'

'Go ahead.'

'Have you noticed anyone following you recently?'

'Funny you should say that,' I said, and told Leah about the phone calls, the camera noises on the last day of term, the person hiding in Memorial Park the day that Nick and I finished, the figure I'd seen in Cosham Avenue the previous Saturday.

'Oh, God!' Leah said. She interlaced her fingers and squeezed so hard that her knuckles showed white. 'They found you. Once they were sure that you still lived in Frinley they only had to wait. They knew I'd show up. It's a threat. If I don't toe the line, they'll hurt the people I care about.'

'Hold on, I'm not following this,' I said. 'Who are *they*?'

'I can't tell you, Danni. It would put you in as much danger as I am.'

'I feel like I'm already in danger. It would be a lot less confusing if I knew why.'

Leah chewed her bottom lip and sighed.

'All right, but you mustn't tell anybody else – not your parents or anyone.'

That brought back some memories.

'Agreed,' I said.

As she talked, Leah was literally twitchy. Tension came off her in waves.

'Have you heard of the Morgans?' she said.

'No. Should I?'

'They're an East End family. They own gambling clubs and a chain of porno shops.'

'You mean they're gangsters?'

'Big-time gangsters,' Leah said. 'Like the Kray brothers, but better at not getting caught. Anyone who gets in their way has a nasty habit of disappearing.'

'And?'

Leah's voice dropped to a murmur.

'My mother is Leo Morgan's granddaughter,' she said. 'She was brought up in Leo's house. She knows where the bodies are buried.'

'Bodies?'

'Victims of gangland hits. Mum's nothing like the rest of her family. She tried to get away from them when she married Dad, but she knows too much about the Morgans for them to let her. They've been hunting us for as long as I can remember. You have no idea what it's like living on the run, Danni. There's this huge weight dangling over us, and it could come down at any time.'

'So why are the Morgans giving me grief? I don't know anything.'

'It's the way they work,' Leah said. 'The Morgans intimidate anybody we get too friendly with. They want to isolate us, to try and force us back into the family.'

'Can't you ask for police protection or something?'

'If the Morgans saw the police hanging around, they'd think that Mum was grassing them up, and they'd get rid of her.'

The amateur psychiatrist in me went to work. Leah's childish imagination hadn't been able to cope with the stress she'd been under, so she'd demonised the people who'd threatened her family and turned them into werewolves, fantasy monsters stalking the dark.

'Is that why you left Frinley so suddenly?' I said.

Leah nodded. 'The Morgans were too close for

comfort, like they are now.'

'What do I do?' I said.

'Sit tight. I'll call Dad. He'll know what to do. He knows some people who might be able to get the Morgans off your back.' Leah looked at her watch. 'I'd better go now. You'll be safer if I'm out of the way.'

At the front door I said, 'How come you didn't call your dad yesterday?'

'I wasn't sure yesterday,' said Leah, 'but after what you just told me...I'm sorry you had to get mixed up in all this, Danni. I promise I'll do my best to make things right. As soon as I have any news, I'll let you know.'

The phone call came half an hour after Leah left. As soon as I put the receiver to my ear, I heard breathing, and outdoor noises in the background that suggested a public call box.

After ten seconds I slammed down the receiver, praying that Leah kept her promise quickly, because I wasn't sure how much more I could take. I recalled another time that I'd felt that way and I shivered, because my memories were taking me closer and closer to what I'd blocked out.

18

I remembered how my anger ran out when I saw the Grey Horse, and my courage ran out with it. The pub was still strung with Christmas fairy-lights, but they didn't make the place seem festive or welcoming; in fact it looked like a haunted house with a ghost in every room. Above the roof, the darkening sky was filled with clouds that promised more snow.

The urge to turn around and forget what I'd come for was tremendously strong, but I knew that if I backed down now, Leah would win and I'd never be free of her.

I crossed the car park and went past Simba's cage. He crouched low, ears down and hackles up, teeth bared in a rattling snarl.

'Good dog, Simba!' I said in a quavering voice.

Another voice said, 'Easy, Simba!'

The dog immediately quietened, stood up and wagged his tail.

Sean came out of the shadows. He pressed his hand against the wire of the cage and Simba licked his fingers, whimpering.

'Thanks,' I said.

'No worries,' said Sean. 'Simba's all right with me – aren't you, boy? You just got to know how to handle him.'

It was the first time I'd talked to Sean. He was surprisingly ordinary, except that he wouldn't make eye contact with me. Even when he turned his face towards me, his eyes didn't point in my direction.

'Are you fond of dogs?' I said.

'Yeah! When I'm older, I'm going on a dog-handling course so I can get a job as a security guard.'

'Security guard?' I said.

Sean smiled. His teeth were as sharp as Leah's.

'I want to work nights,' he said. 'I like the dark.'

'Er, is Leah at home?'

'I expect.'

'Is she ill, or...?'

'Who cares?' said Sean.

I left him petting Simba, and went to ring the back-door bell.

Mr Warner opened the door.

'Come in out of the cold,' he said. 'How's tricks?'

'Fine,' I said, stepping inside. 'I wondered how Leah was. She wasn't at school today.'

Mr Warner frowned.

'Wasn't she? Oh, no, that's right. She had one of her headaches. Migraine. She gets them bad.'

Mrs Warner bustled out of a back room, wiping her hands on a tea towel.

'Hello there, Danni!' she said. 'Come to cheer up the invalid? Can I get you a warm drink? You must be perished.'

'No thank you,' I said. 'I can't stay for long.'

'Did you walk all the way?'

'Yes.'

'Couldn't you have caught a bus?'

'I thought walking would be warmer than standing at a bus stop.'

'Public transport's a disgrace in this town,' said Mr Warner. 'The local authority ought to get its act together.'

Mr and Mrs Warner were side by side. They had identical fixed smiles and empty eyes; it was eerie.

'Is Leah in her room?' I asked.

'Been there all day,' said Mrs Warner. 'She was feeling a bit poorly.'

'I told Danni about Leah's migraine,' said Mr Warner.

'That's right, a migraine,' Mrs Warner said. 'The doctors can't do anything for her. She has to lie in bed with the curtains drawn and wait until it goes away. Terrible things, migraines.'

'They must be,' I said.

'D'you suffer from them, Danni?'

'No.'

'You should count yourself lucky. I wouldn't wish them on my worst enemy.'

'Me neither,' said Mr Warner. 'Not migraines.'

Something odd was happening. It was as if Mr and Mrs Warner were talking in a code that I didn't understand, and they were trying so hard to act normally that it was weird.

'I'll go on up to Leah's room, shall I?' I said.

'Yes, do,' said Mrs Warner. 'She'll be ever so pleased to see you. Don't worry if she seems a bit...well, you know. It'll be the migraine.'

'They take different people different ways,' Mr

Warner said.

On my way to the staircase, I glanced over my shoulder. Mr and Mrs Warner were standing in the same position, the same smiles still on their faces, like robots that someone had forgotten to disconnect.

When I reached the door of Leah's room I took a deep breath, knocked and said, 'Leah? It's me.'

'Come in, Danni.'

The only light in the room was a small candle burning on Leah's bedside table. She was lying on the bed, dressed in black jeans and a black sweatshirt.

'How's the migraine?' I said.

'I know what you've come to say,' said Leah.

'You do?'

'You've come to tell me you don't want to be friends with me any more. I don't deserve to be your friend after what I did, and you're right. I knew it was wrong, but I couldn't stop myself. I want to be your best friend – not Rose! You don't know how important you are to me, Danni. You're the only person who ever—'

Her shoulders shook. Tears slid down her face, gleaming in the candle-light.

'I'm not a toy, Leah,' I said. 'You don't own me. I can have other friends if I want to.'

'I know.'

'I wanted to be friends with you *and* Rose.'

'I'm horrible!' Leah sobbed. 'I can't help it. When I get angry I say nasty things. I don't know how to be a good friend. Not many people like me, and if someone ever does, we have to move soon after. I never get to be close to anyone. No one cares about me.'

'Your family does.'

Leah blew her nose into a tissue.

'Families don't count, do they?' she said. 'Anyway, I get on their nerves too. I don't blame you for wanting to break up with me, Danni. I'm horrible.'

'Don't keep saying that!'

'Why not – it's true, isn't it? I was meant to be on my own. I'm the only person who can stand me.'

She was drawing me in, making me feel that it was my fault her feelings were hurt.

'Leah—' I said.

Leah held up a hand to stop me.

'It's all right, Danni,' she said. 'There's something I've got to do, and it's better if I do it alone. Go home and let me get on with it.'

'You don't have to do anything alone, Leah,' I said.

'I'm your friend. I might not be the best friend in the world, but—'

'I know where the werewolf's lair is,' Leah said. 'I know where he's hiding. I'm sick of running, so I'm going there tomorrow to meet him face to face.'

My guilt vanished. I saw that Leah had been manipulating me, all her tears had been part of an act. She hadn't been able to buy my friendship, so she'd tried to blackmail it out of me. It was so pathetic that I felt sorry for her, but I made up my mind to put a stop to the werewolf stories once and for all, and decided to try a little manipulation of my own.

'Where is it?' I said.

'Huh?'

'The werewolf's lair.'

'Memorial Park.'

'But Memorial Park has been shut up for years! No one goes there.'

'Exactly,' said Leah. 'The perfect place for a werewolf to take his victims.'

I thought I had it sussed: this was the part where I was supposed to beg Leah not to go to the park, and the begging would show how much I cared about her. Instead, I said, 'I'll come with you.'

Leah's face lit up.

'Would you really do that for me?' she said.

'Sure,' I said. 'That's what friends are for.'

I was sure that I'd trapped her. I'd pushed her right to the edge of the werewolf game. Once we were in the park, she wouldn't be able to keep up the pretence. She'd be forced to admit that the werewolves were only make-believe, and provide me with an excuse to break off our friendship. I even imagined my exit line – *I don't want to be friends with a liar!* – and looked forward to delivering it.

'I have to go now,' I said. 'My mum doesn't know I'm here. I want to be home before she gets in and starts worrying.'

'My dad can give you a lift,' said Leah.

'It's OK, I'll catch the bus. What time tomorrow?'

'Meet me outside Memorial Hall at two o' clock,' said Leah. 'Don't wear any bright clothes or perfume. Werewolves have sharp eyesight and sense of smell.'

Her yellow eyes were glowing triumphantly, and for a split-second I wondered who was bluffing whom.

19

After the anonymous call, believe it or not, I dozed off on the sofa. It must have been a self-defence thing: my mind used sleep as a bolt-hole to escape from all the thoughts that were skidding around it. I had a confusing dream made up of fragments of the day and old memories.

In the dream, I was at a party that was being held in the supermarket. Nick, Rose and Simon were there, chatting and laughing, sipping champagne from tall glasses. The supermarket was still open; customers passed to and fro pushing loaded trolleys. I was trying to avoid conversation, because I was dressed in my junior school uniform and it would be embarrassing if anyone noticed. David kept popping up from behind the shelving racks, his camera flashing and buzzing.

Suddenly I saw a wolf at the far end of the aisle, its

red tongue lolling as it padded towards me, its shadow sliding across the floor tiles.

I said to David, 'Should that thing be loose in here?'

David said, 'Chill, Danni. It's only Leah. The party was her idea.'

I looked at the wolf again and saw that it *was* Leah; the wolf had been inside her all along...

I woke with a start, my brain super-clear. Nothing that Leah had told me actually hung together – gangland killings, East End heavies waiting at bus stops in Frinley – it was ludicrous, like the plot of a hundred TV cop shows, and Leah had almost suckered me in to believing it, just like she'd almost made me believe in werewolves when we were kids. Why, after all those years, would anyone think that I was still important enough to her for hurting me to be used as a threat against her? The only person who could possibly have known about Leah's coming to see me was Leah herself.

She was the one who'd made the calls; she was the one who'd photographed me on the last day of term. I'd assumed that the hooded figure on Cosham Avenue had been a man, but it could have been Leah. She was the wolf who'd been stalking me. Then she'd woven a fantasy and given me the starring role – Danni, the helpless female. But why had she done it – did she want revenge for some reason?

'Bitch!' I said aloud.

I should have twigged at that point how disturbed and irrational Leah was, but I was too angry to be sympathetic. I remembered that old saying, 'Don't get mad, get even,' and I began to plan how. I could have contacted the police and had her picked up, but that would've been too impersonal. It would be far more satisfying to confront Leah in person, see the look of shame on her face when she confessed. I was going to have it out with her, like I should have that Christmas, and finish our unfinished business.

All I had to do was wait. Leah was bound to ring me and suggest a meeting – instinct even told me the place she'd choose – and I'd go along with her, letting her think that she was in control. Turning the tables on her would be sweet, a moment to savour.

How could I have been such a dork?

I slept in late on Saturday morning. When I went downstairs, Mum and Dad were gathering shopping bags for their weekly assault on the hypermarket.

'Afternoon,' said Dad. 'I was just about to find a Prince Charming to kiss you awake.'

'You would've had a long search,' I said.

'Will you be going out later, Danielle?' Mum asked.

'Maybe,' I said. 'I'm expecting a friend to ring me.'

'You'd better take an umbrella with you. It's filthy out there.'

Mum wasn't exaggerating. When I glanced through the kitchen window while I was having breakfast, I saw that the sky was covered with inky black clouds. The weather was about to change at last and we were in for a dramatic storm; the air was going to get cleared in more ways than one.

The call came at one o'clock. I let the phone ring three times so that it wouldn't seem like I was standing over it – which I was.

'Danni?' said Leah.

I had to give it to her, she had the voice just right, anxious and slightly breathless.

'Hi,' I said. 'I'm glad you rang. I hardly got any sleep last night.'

'Me neither. I was worrying about you.'

Liar! I thought.

Leah said, 'Listen, I talked to my dad first thing,

and he knows how we can get this mess sorted.'

'How?'

'I don't want to say on the phone. Could we meet up at two o'clock?'

'Sure,' I said. 'Whereabouts?'

'Memorial Park?'

My instinct had been right.

'I'll be there,' I said. 'But it's not the same as it used to be. The council got a grant from the Millennium Fund to do it up. It's really pretty now.'

'I know. I went there the other day for old times' sake. It was our special place, wasn't it?'

I twitched. Had it been her in the bushes the time I was in the park with Nick? My anger went up a notch, but I managed to keep my voice calm and said, 'It certainly was. I'm looking forward to seeing you there.'

'Don't be frightened, will you, Danni?' Leah said. 'I won't let anything happen to you.'

When I put down the receiver, I had a big, smug smile on my face.

The storm broke the moment I stepped outside. Sheet-lightning flashed across the sky, thunder growled and the rain came down in fat drops. The spokes of my umbrella streamed water on to my jacket, and my socks were soaked before I reached the front gate. I was the only person in the street. Everybody else was too sensible to be out. Gutters and drains flooded. Passing traffic drenched me with dirty water, but I hardly noticed; facing Leah with the truth was more important to me than staying dry.

I made the park with two minutes to spare. There was no sign of Leah. I walked through the gates and glanced over at the shelter, but it was empty. I headed for it, so that I could get out of the rain. The path ran near a clump of fir trees, and I caught their pine scent on the damp air.

Then an arm came from behind, grabbing me around the neck. A hand pressed a cloth to my face. Chemical fumes stung my eyes. The world turned red. In the centre of the redness was a black circle that pulsed. With each pulse the circle grew wider, until at last it was big enough to swallow me. I fell down into the dark, and time ran back, and back, and back to the memory I'd buried deepest.

20

When I was a kid, Memorial Park was a local legend. No one knew for sure why it had been shut down. Stories gathered around it like cobwebs, but nobody was certain which story was true, or if any of them were. Some said it had been too popular with courting couples looking for somewhere to make out on Saturday night, others said that burglars had used it as a back way in to a builder's merchants; the creepiest story said that a series of murders had taken place there. For whatever reason, the park had a bad reputation.

And it looked like a place with a bad reputation. The front gates, and the padlock and chain that secured them, were badly rusted. Thickets of brambles threw out runners armed with terrifying spikes over the tops of the low walls that surrounded it. Red trunked fir trees with dark green foliage had grown so tall that they cast a gloom all year round. Even in the hot sunshine of midsummer, Memorial Park was a blot of shadow living in its own personal season. As far as potential locations for a werewolf's lair went in Frinley, Leah had chosen the best.

The weather was fine that Saturday – one of those bright winter days that look summery until you step outside and the cold numbs your fingers. Leah was already waiting at Memorial Hall when I arrived. She looked like a terrorist: dressed in black, the hood of her jacket pulled up, a scarf wrapped around the lower half of her face.

'I thought you might change your mind,' she said.

Thought or hoped?

'Well I didn't and I'm here,' I said. 'How are we going to do this?'

Leah pointed across Memorial Road.

'There's a gap in the brambles over there,' she said. 'We'll go in that way. Here.'

She offered me a closed clasp-knife with a bone handle.

'No thanks!' I said.

'You might need it.'

'I won't. If anything happens, I'll just run. I'm not fighting anyone.'

Leah fixed me with her eyes.

'I'd feel safer if you had a knife,' she said. 'I'm the one who got you into this, so take it for my sake.'

Reluctantly, I slipped the knife into the back pocket of my jeans, and as far as I was concerned it was staying right there.

We crossed the road, looked around to check that no one was in sight, clambered over the wall and dropped down.

The silence was immediate: no traffic, no birds singing, just a high whine in my ears and the beat of my pulse.

'Follow me,' said Leah.

She crouched and went forward, holding back branches for me. A minute or two later we came out into the open.

To our left was a tennis court; weeds had punched their way right through the tarmac, then withered, leaving behind the sweetish smell of rotting vegetables. Straight ahead lay a small shelter. To our right stood a battered wooden sign that began, *A person shall not —— in the pleasure park.* The rest of the message was illegible flakes of old paint.

'This way,' Leah said.

She led me over to the shelter. Inside there were stone stumps that had once been benches. The walls were crazed with graffiti : *MUFC*; *CHELSEA MUST DIE*; *DO DRAW AND GET STONED*. Small stalactites on the ceiling dripped like running noses. In the centre of the floor was a mound of ash surrounded by a ragged black patch.

'This is where he makes a fire when he gets cold,' said Leah, her voice echoing off the walls. She took me over to a corner and showed me a scatter of dried bones. 'He's eaten a baby,' she said.

The bones looked more like the remains of a KFC takeaway to me, but I didn't say anything.

'Can you feel him?' Leah said.

I could feel something. The strangeness of the park had seeped into me. It had been abandoned and forgotten so totally that it had no connection with the world outside. Anything seemed possible there, even werewolves.

'Look!' said Leah.

She tapped the floor with the toe of her trainer. I saw a mark in the grime. It looked like the paw print of a large dog, but it was too blurred for me to be sure.

My thoughts came in a rush. Had Leah set all this up: lit a fire, dumped chicken bones, let Simba loose to roam around and leave tracks? Or was she making it up as she went along, taking the things she came across and working them into her dream world?

'Why here?' I said. 'If werewolves look ordinary, why doesn't he book into a guest house?'

'I told you,' said Leah. 'He brings his victims here.'

'Leah, if a werewolf kidnapped and ate a baby, wouldn't the parents call the police?'

'The police and the press are in on it. They don't want people to know about werewolves, because it would cause a panic. The government keeps secret files. Scientists use werewolf genes in experiments. They're trying to breed a race of superhumans.'

'Come off it, Leah!' I said. 'I've seen *The X-Files* too.'

'What d'you mean?'

'I mean you're making all this up. You don't really think that I believe it, do you?'

Leah took something out of her jacket pocket. There was a sharp click, and a knife blade sprang out of her clenched fist.

'Believe what you like,' she said. 'I'm going hunting.'

She took a step towards me and I thought she was going to attack me – like she was so jealous of me and Rose that she was going to fix it so I couldn't be friends with anybody – but she brushed past, heading for a clump of pine trees.

I lasted five seconds on my own before I went after her.

'Leah, can we stop and talk about this,' I said.

Leah just kept walking stubbornly ahead.

'If you've got some kind of problem, you can tell me.'

Leah stopped walking and glared at me.

'You think I'm mad, don't you?' she said.

Which is precisely what I thought, but I wasn't going to let on while she was holding a knife.

'I think you're upset and it's stressing you out,' I said. 'Can't you tell me about it?'

'I already did, and look where it got me!' said Leah. 'You blabbed to Rose about me, didn't you? Even though you promised not to. You reckoned that the promise didn't count because it was only me. I bet the two of you had a good laugh, didn't you?'

'No. It wasn't like that.'

'Then what was it like?'

I kept my eyes on the knife. Reflected sunshine from the blade dazzled me.

'Rose thinks you need help and so do I,' I said.

There was a rustling sound. Leah and I turned simultaneously towards a bank of laurel bushes. The green leaves were streaked with yellow, as though the plants had contracted a disease.

I stared hard. Was it the wind twitching the leaves, or was someone huddled there, watching? I thought I heard the sound of heavy breathing.

'He's there!' screeched Leah.

My nerve snapped. Panic pushed me back past the shelter and into the undergrowth. Twigs lashed me, thorns snagged on my jacket and jeans. I scrabbled over the wall and ran blindly across Memorial Road; then I paused and looked back.

Leah was on the pavement opposite. There was mud on her jacket. She'd taken off her scarf and she was smiling at me, her right hand raised to show me the knife. The blade was red; the redness had streaked her fingers.

'See?' she said.

'I don't see anything!' I said. 'I don't want to see

anything! Leave me alone, Leah!'

I turned my back on her and ran for home as fast as
I could go.

Later on that evening, when I'd calmed down, I began
to think logically – or I went into denial. There hadn't
been a werewolf in Memorial Park, more like a dosser
sleeping rough. The red stuff on Leah's hand hadn't
been blood, just lipstick or maybe ketchup to fool me.
The whole thing had been a complicated sick joke,
and I'd fallen for it. I'd had it with Leah and at eight
o' clock I rang the Grey Horse to tell her so.

An unfamiliar voice answered.

'Can I speak to Leah?' I said.

'Sorry, they've gone.'

'Who?'

'The Warners. The whole family have packed up
and done a runner.'

'Where have they gone?'

'Your guess is as good as mine, but they've left the
place in a right mess.'

'Are you a friend of theirs?'

The person on the other end laughed.

'No, I'm the muggins from the brewery who has to

clear up after them. The Warners are no friends of mine.'

On Sunday, I got Dad to give me a lift to the Grey Horse so that I could see whether what I'd been told was true. The black car with tinted windows was missing from the car park, Simba's cage was empty, the shutters on the windows were closed and there was a notice stuck to the front door: *Opening shortly under new management.*

Leah and her family had vanished.

21

Light slowly seeped back into the darkness, turning it grey. I dry-heaved, coughing and spluttering as I fought to catch my breath. My vision cleared, but I didn't recognise what I was seeing: blobs of white on a brown background scattered with ginger threads. Then the threads became dried pine-needles; the brown, damp earth; the white blobs were trainers with gold laces.

I raised my head. I was in the clump of fir trees, and Leah was smiling down at me. Her canine teeth gleamed. Her eyes were sly and alert. She'd had her hair restyled and dyed, and it took me a few seconds to realise that it was the same as mine.

'How are you feeling?' she said.

I tried to stand and couldn't. My ankles were tied with plastic-coated washing line and my wrists were fastened behind my back.

'Untie me,' I said, my voice booming in my ears.

'The giddiness will go away soon,' said Leah. 'It's good gear, isn't it? I scored it from a guy in a night-club.'

I couldn't make out much of what she was saying. Her words didn't mean anything.

'It's worked out perfectly, hasn't it?' said Leah. 'You must be as pleased as I am. We couldn't have asked for better weather. The rain kept everybody else away, so it's just you and I.'

'It was you who followed me round and rang me up, wasn't it?' I said.

Leah laughed.

'So you finally worked it out!' she said. 'I wondered how long it would take you. I've been tracking you for ages. I wanted things to be right, and they are.'

'So that guff about the Morgans—?'

'It wasn't guff. Mum was in a witness protection scheme but she's out of danger now. If I hadn't put in some true stuff, you wouldn't have believed me.'

I'd seen clumsy Leah and graceful Leah; this was Leah the wolf, ultra-aware and running on instinct.

Fear pressed against my bladder.

'Why, Leah?' I said.

'The voices.'

'What voices?'

'The werewolves. My therapist said that I'd stop hearing them when I achieved closure and I did for a while. Then, after Marty dumped me, I got really down, you know? I did a lot of drugs, I can't remember how many, I took everything I could get my hands on – uppers, downers, you name it. They helped for a bit, but then the voices came back. It was like being little again. When my parents told me I mustn't make any friends, I thought it was because there was something wrong with me, that it was my fault people were after us. It was my fault about Marty, too. I just wasn't good enough for him. The werewolves told me that I was the one to blame and I had to be punished. It was really scary, Danni.'

Right at that moment, I could have told Leah a thing or two about being scared, but instead I tried to buy myself some time.

'Leah,' I said, 'why don't you untie me so we can talk this through together?'

Leah glanced at me as though I were a small child who'd asked a stupid question.

'I don't need to talk,' she said. 'I'm not scared any more. I've found a way of hiding from the werewolves for ever. It's so simple, I'm amazed I never thought of it before.' She squatted down and looked me straight in the eyes. 'I can escape if I change into someone else, and I'm going to change into you, Danni. Don't you see? You're the person I always should have been. That's why your friendship was so important to me. I used to think you could help me find a way out of my problems, but all the time you *were* the way out, only I was too young to realise. I'll live in your house, sleep in your bed, wear your clothes, go to your school and I'll be so you that no one will notice.'

'You can't do that!' I said.

'Yes I can. I've already started. Nick will be my boyfriend, and I'll two-time him with David. Your parents will soon get used to having me round the place. Of course, I'll have to get rid of you first. There can't be two Dannis, can there? I know you won't mind, because you'll be helping me to be free, and we both want to be free, don't we?'

'Listen to me, Leah,' I said. 'You're not thinking straight. All those drugs you took have confused you. Everybody will know that you're not me because we're different. If you hurt me, you'll get yourself into trouble. You'll be put away somewhere for years. What kind of freedom is that?'

Leah frowned.

'Hurt you? I could never hurt you, Danni.' She brought a knife out of the pocket of her silk baseball-jacket. The blade had a curved point. 'It'll be quick, I promise. There'll be hardly any pain – only a scratch. It'll be like falling asleep. Afterwards I'll bury you here. I'm glad it's here, aren't you? This is our place.'

Reason hadn't worked, so I tried shock-tactics.

'You're talking murder, Leah!' I said harshly.

'No, it's not murder. I'm borrowing your life so I can be happy. You'll be happy too, sleeping like a princess.'

I yelled as loudly as I could. There were no words in the yell; I sounded like a desperate animal caught in a trap. I thought I heard something, like an answering cry or an echo.

'Don't fuss, Danni,' Leah scolded. 'I've researched it on the internet. If I cut you here,' she pointed to a spot on her neck, 'you'll bleed to death in ninety seconds. Count to ninety and it'll be over. That's not long, is it? Not when you compare it to a lifetime.'

Half of me was jibbering with panic, the other half was strangely calm. I imagined what it was going to be like: the sting of the knife; my strength draining away; the black silence. Like most people, I'd wondered when and where my death would happen and here it was, in Leah's wolf-eyes and smile, in the brightness of the blade she stretched out towards me...

There was a crash in the undergrowth. Someone pushed me aside and kicked the knife out of Leah's hand. I heard grunts and swearing.

I moved myself into a better position, and saw two figures struggling. One was Leah, the other was Nick. Nick had his arms wrapped tightly around her. Leah struggled and strained, her face red with effort. Then she drew back her head and butted Nick on the bridge of the nose. Nick relaxed his grip; Leah broke loose and scrambled away.

Nick swayed. He sat heavily on the ground next to me. Blood streamed out of his nose, down over his top lip.

'Don't let her get away, Nick!' I said.

'She won't get far,' said Nick. He pulled a mobile phone from the pocket of his jeans, dialled a number and said, 'Police, please.'

I started crying and couldn't stop.

Nick finished his call and cradled me in his arms. I sobbed into his coat. We must have looked peculiar, sheltering in the trees like two lost children in a fairy story.

Leah was taken into custody two hours later. She was arrested at Frinley station, where she'd been waiting for a train to take her to London. After she'd been charged, she was sent to a secure psychiatric unit.

For me, what followed was a blur of policemen and solicitors, and a series of statements that went over the same stuff again and again.

The first time Nick and I met after that afternoon in Memorial Park, his nose was swollen to twice its normal size, and his voice sounded as if he had a heavy cold. Luckily for me, Rose had warned him that Leah couldn't be trusted and might possibly turn nasty, so he'd ignored what I'd said about keeping watch, and he'd followed me through the storm. He saw me go into the park, waited for me to come out, and when he heard me shouting, he came in after me.

'You were incredibly brave!' I said.

'I didn't have time to think about being brave,'

said Nick. 'I just reacted.'

'Leah could have stabbed you.'

'I know. That's why I disarmed her first.'

'You saved my life.'

'Maybe. D'you think she actually would have gone through with it?'

I'd asked myself the same question a million times.

'I don't know,' I said, 'but I'm grateful that I didn't find out. Leah was obsessed with me, Nick, she might have done anything.'

'I know how that feels.'

'It's like she wanted to be me so much, she believed she could do it.'

'She needs specialist help, Danni, and I'm sure she'll get it now.'

'You think so?'

Nick nodded.

'One of the policemen who interviewed me said that he didn't think Leah would be fit to plead to any charges,' he said. 'He reckoned that a psychiatrist would recommend her to a secure hospital somewhere. She won't be bothering you again – and at least one good thing's come out of this. If they hold a Cyrano de Bergerac lookalike-competition, I'm odds on favourite.'

'Two good things,' I said.

'Huh?'

I took Nick's face in my hands and kissed him.

'Ouch!' he said. 'What was that for?'

'Nick, if I promise not to be a cow, and not to take you for granted or order you about, is there any chance that we could—?'

'No promises,' said Nick. 'We'll take things as they come and see how it goes.'

I still have scars. I jump whenever the phone rings, and I won't go near unlit places at night. I had recurring dreams that Leah was out there, lurking in the shadows to grab me, but lately the dreams have altered. Leah and I meet in the light. We talk and she's changed, become the happy person she longed to be. Perhaps one day, when she's finally cured, that's what will happen. Sometimes I try to reach her with my mind, find the lonely kid who hated herself so much that she wanted to be someone else. I never quite make it though. I guess we can only be who we are.

I don't know if I'll ever see Leah again, or how I'd feel about it if I did. I'd like to think that I could forgive her, but I'm not sure. The peculiar thing is that

Leah changed me, changed the personality she was going to take as her own. I'm more cautious of people I don't know and more appreciative of the people I do know, like Rose and Nick. Nick and I may not always be an item, but we'll always be friends. The bond between us is too strong to break.

In a weird kind of way, I owe Leah a lot.

More Black Apples
to get your teeth into...

Also by Andrew Matthews

1 84121 758 1   £4.99

'Anna? I'd like you to meet Pete.'
Anna turned, and her breath was taken away.
Pete was beautiful.

Pete may be gorgeous, but he's very unfriendly.
And anyway, Anna's got other things on her mind.
Sent away for the summer to stop her seeing
her boyfriend, Anna is pining for her lost love.

At first.

But then she gets involved in the local wolf
sanctuary, and discovers a thrilling and dangerous
passion. A passion that eventually throws her
and Pete together in a time of crisis.

Jean Ure

1 84121 831 6   £4.99

Joel's brother, Noah, is a real heart-throb, always
dating different girls. But when Lars Kennedy turns
up, things seem to change. Tall, blond and gorgeous,
everyone falls for Lars – even Joel's mum!

Then comes a startling revelation. One that will
have fatal consequences...but will also be the start
of a new life.

A powerful and moving story guaranteed to grip
you from start to finish.

'A fun, fab read. It will pull on those heartstrings.'
Mizz

Michael Coleman

1 84121 161 3   £4.99

Ever heard of a Readathon?
Well, Robbie and his mates have
come up with something much
more exciting: a snogathon! But
it's top secret. Imagine how the
girls would feel to know they're
being ranked by snogability!

Robbie wants to win the
competition by snogging Mel,
the class ice maiden. But Mel might just have other ideas...

A story of laughs, love, lessons...and snogging!

Also by Michael Coleman

Tag

1 86039 654 2   £4.99

'A riveting combination of suspense and thrills.' *Boox*

'An intensely powerful and well-written story with a palpable
sense of danger and suspense.' *The School Librarian*

Weirdo's War

1 86039 812 X   £3.99

Shortlisted for the Carnegie Medal, the Lancashire
Children's Book Award and the Writers Guild Award

'Tense and psychological.' *The Times*

Bernard Ashley

1 84121 814 6   £4.99

Marsh End. Lonely, isolated and bleak, Sophia's mum loves it.

But for Sophia, the brooding skies hold no solace for her lost father, or her lost life in London. Nothing ever happens in this dead end place.

That is until Revenge House begins to reveal its murky secrets, and Sophia and her mum find themselves sucked into a brutal criminal underworld that will eventually threaten their lives.

Also by Bernard Ashley

Little Soldier
1 86039 879 0   £4.99

Shortlisted for the Carnegie Medal and the *Guardian* Children's Fiction Award

'So pacy that it is difficult to turn the pages fast enough.'
The School Librarian

Tiger Without Teeth
1 86039 605 4   £4.99

Shortlisted for the Sheffield Children's Book Award and the Angus Award.

'Bernard Ashley's great gift is to turn what seems to be low-key realism into something much stronger and more resonant.'
Philip Pullman

ORCHARD BLACK APPLES

All priced at £4.99

Orchard Black Apples are available from all good bookshops,
or can be ordered direct from the publisher:
Orchard Books, PO BOX 29, Douglas IM99 1BQ
Credit card orders please telephone 01624 836000
or fax 01624 837033or visit our Internet site: www.wattspub.co.uk
or e-mail: bookshop@enterprise.net for details.

To order please quote title, author and ISBN
and your full name and address.
Cheques and postal orders should be made payable to 'Bookpost plc.'
Postage and packing is FREE within the UK
(overseas customers should add £1.00 per book).

Prices and availability are subject to change.